I0665060

This is a work of fiction. If it sounds real, well, that's what a writer does. If you think one of the characters is based on you then be flattered. Nobody else will suspect unless you tell them, and you're free to tell as many people as you like, as long as you buy each of them at least one copy, if not two.

All names were changed to protect the innocent, guilty, or the author.

THANKS

To my friends and family who are there for me. In geographical order, including, but not limited to: Debra, Celeste, Max, Tim, Jimmie, Dora, Fred, Susan, David, Phil, Lorenzo, Bruce, Lisa, Loren, Ocea, Ari, Mike, Violet, Jett, Jack, and David. Thanks to my writing group who kept me going and kept it real: Robert, Greg, Christopher, Jeremy, Jennie and Karin. And Erin for her editing and proofing skills!

THE WEEKEND BOYFRIEND

CHARACTERS

David - 41, successful screenwriter, formerly married to Tedd.

Lawrence - 28, East Indian, Geology/Gemology PhD student. In love with David.

Tedd - 41, male-model looks, fashion designer, formerly married to David, can't keep it in his pants.

Jez- David and Lawrence's couples counselor who ~~sleeps with~~ Tedd.

Dory - David and Lawrence's therapist. 50s, divorced.

Shelli - 65, widowed billionairess. David's friend and confidant who thinks of him as the gay son she never had.

HIROTO – 55, BISEXUAL JAPANESE BUTLER/LOVER TO SHELLI WHO HE MET IN THE PEACE CORPS.

Yasmin – 28, East Indian. Lawrence's best friend who wants more from him.

Cheyenne - 24, cowboy. Lawrence's lover in Wyoming.

Cubby - 32, non-binary fashion designer. David's short-term boyfriend.

Zorn - 500,000 year old Alien in David's "Stunning Aliens" script who has a life of his own in David's mind.

Norz - Female alien in David's script.

J. Michael - Successful plagiarist writer.

Marc - Producer of Clean Comedies that David writes.

Leif - 40, Male nurse, Swedish, muscle man - Screenwriter of "*Trollheim*."

Oscar - 63, White, head of production at Universal who oversees production on "*Trollheim*."

TARSEM – 45, EAST INDIAN, DIRECTOR OF "*TROLLHEIM*."

Harry - 35, Latino, grip on "*Trollheim*" movie production and David's short-term assistant and lover.

RASHID – YASMIN'S HAIRDRESSER LOVER.

Azad - 58, Yasmin's father, East Indian, owns a dry cleaning business.

Laila – 53, East Indian – Lawrence's mother.

Bashir - 55, East Indian - Lawrence's father.

Fareed – 55, East Indian – Lawrence's gay uncle (Bashir's twin brother).

Rhu - 30, Asian, *silent* Buddhist monk.

Minister - presides~ over the wedding.

Diane Keaton - herself - Starring in "Trollheim" as Mrs. Claus.

Robert Pattinson - himself - Starring in "Trollheim"

AND SO IT BEGINS...

DAVID

I can't write when I'm happy—that's a problem for a writer. Dory, my therapist, said I should write about this belief—to prove myself wrong. She said, and I quote, "you can turn your past shit into future fertilizer." She's profound that way.

She said it would help me see how I lost the love of my life, Lawrence, who wasn't my husband. Tedd was my husband. We'd been together for 22 happy-ish years, though married just a year before I found him in bed with another man. Not just another man, our couples counselor, Jez. I suspected Jez would be trouble because he looked too handsome with his colorful cardigans and studied pipe smoking. I'd had my share of fantasies about him which I chalked up to "projections" but clearly Tedd wanted Jez to project into him personally.

The irony is that we'd been talking about opening up our relationship. Jez had told us that the key to this was *honesty*. Honestly, that's what he said. If Tedd had said, "Davey," (he was the only one who ever called me *Davey*) "Davey, let's open our relationship and bring Jez in," I would have said, "It sounds unethically delightful."

My only question would have been, "Can I wear his colorful sweaters?" Because, being totally honest, I found it hard to focus on anything Jez said because I wanted to know where he got his sweaters. When I asked, he said, "A counselor needs to keep some things private," which made me want to kick him in the balls and run away with his sweater, but I've never been good at either kicking or running.

Now that I remembered what he said, that was another red flag, right? He was keeping more than his sweater private.

When I found Tedd and Jez together, the first thing I did was take my clothes off and get in bed with them. After all, weren't they there waiting for me to complete the sexy threesome?

It dawned on me this *wasn't* the case when Jez started crying and Tedd said, and I quote, "this isn't what it looks like."

I might have forgiven him if he hadn't said that clichéd line, but as a writer, a bad line was unforgivable. Seriously, what else could it have been? I know—it started as a counseling session, but then both of them got very hot—and sleepy—so they had to take off all their clothes and go to bed. Sure, that must have been what Tedd would have told me, if I'd stayed to listen.

Instead, I got out of bed, farted at them (it wasn't a conscious move, it's not like I had a superpower, though that would have been useful), grabbed my clothes and Jez's colorful sweater (pink and orange, unfortunately not one of his best), and Tedd's shoes, which were much nicer and more expensive than mine. I ran into the living room, threw on the clothes and ran out of the house carrying the small Picasso lithograph I'd saved up to buy Tedd for our first anniversary because I knew he'd coveted it. If I could have carried more, like the minimalist flatware or the expensive Italian toaster I would have.

I slammed the door, then had an idea and quietly unlocked it, taking Tedd's car keys so I could take Tedd's car, also nicer than mine. Tedd cared about things more than I did. So he had Hunter and Barrow shoes custom made in London for $1,500 a pair while I wore comfortable Skechers that cost $69 at the outlet store. His car was a Jaguar I-pace, the all-electric one, and mine was an 8 year old Fiat 500 I called "Sage" because that's what color it was. I was perfectly happy with it and once I was driving away in his silent car, I felt sorry for my car. I parked the Jag miles away in an iffy part of town, took an Uber back to the house, got my car and left Tedd with nothing.

That's when the barrage of text messages began. Three-a-minute to start. I'd never known Tedd to be a particularly fast typist with his thumbs, so he must have been using the voice transcription, which would also explain the texts that read, "Please cum book, we need to tech." I found it telling that his phone knew the word "cum."

I drove to my friend Shelli's house. Shelli had been a friend to both of us—but she was really *my* friend. I brought her into the relationship, and if I'd been smart enough to have a prenup, I would have added her to the list of things I got exclusively if we broke up.

I didn't have to. As soon as she saw my tears raining down on the ugly, ill-fitting sweater she engulfed me in a huge hug. She gave the best hugs because she had wonderful breasts. It doesn't matter that gay guys aren't sexually attracted to breasts, they're lying if they say they don't love them anyway. And I loved hers. I loved her.

SHELLI

I loved David—he was the gay son I always wanted but never had. I had two sons with two different husbands but they'd both turned out straight and played golf—I was bored to tears!

David and I shopped together. Made bitchy comments about other people's plastic surgery together. Ate too much together. He even had my Rubenesque figure whereas my sons took after their fathers and were stiffly athletic.

I loved David most because he was there for me no matter what. Like when my first husband, Magnus, died when his private jet crashed, leaving me immensely wealthy with a controlling interest in Comcast. Or when my second husband, Simon, died of cancer, leaving me even wealthier with a minority voting block of Tesla.

Or when I had cancer twice. I lost all my hair during chemo and made it my style to always be nearly bald which Andre Leon Talley said I made stunningly chic.

David, bless him, made me laugh—like nobody else could.

DAVID

I couldn't remember all the horrible things that had happened to Shelli at the moment because I was too upset about my one horrible thing. In the past, I was proud to be there for Shelli, making her laugh and making her food. I knit her colorful cashmere hats that Andre Leon Talley said "aspired to kitsch."

I insisted Shelli stay with us when she couldn't face going back to her palatial Bel Air estate alone. I'm not making light of the fact that she was almost obscenely wealthy because she was also as generous as you imagine you'd be if you were rich— like giving $100 tips to everyone (including the people at Starbucks), and donating shit tons of money to charity.

She was also always generous to Tedd and me. When we moved into our tiny little house in unfashionable eastern wilds of West Hollywood she looked around and said, "Oh, honeys, I know you're gay and should genetically have exquisite taste, but you really need a decorator— I'm sending Martyn over to help you."

He made our house like something out of *Architectural Digest* (in fact, it was featured in *Architectural Digest* right after Jennifer Aniston's newest mansion with her latest husband). We had a three-way with him (Martyn, not Jennifer's husband, though we would have if he'd shown the slightest interest).

I especially enjoyed this three-way because Martyn was more into me than Tedd, which once again spoke to his elevated taste level. "You're quite delicious," he told me with his affected English accent.

He wanted to continue to have a thing, but Tedd and I weren't weren't open and *I* wasn't about to fuck around behind Tedd's back or today I might be Mrs. Martyn Bullard, living on the Côte d'Azur amidst a veritable sea of black and white striped decor and dogs that looked like fluffy pillows.

Today I turned to Shelli for comfort and sage advice, or at least chocolates.

SHELLI

David cried all over my Tom Ford kaftan. Tom was my next-door neighbor and made the kaftans especially for me. I could feel

David's tears soaking through the silk satin but couldn't understand what David was sobbing about, other than it had something to do with Tedd, his handsome schmuck of a husband who I told him not to marry in the first place.

DAVID

As my sobbing subsided, I felt bad when I realized that her Tom Ford kaftan was surely dry-clean only. I'd always wanted to have a three-way with Tom but I was too insecure to bring it up. Now that Tedd was no longer in the picture, maybe I'd walk next door and offer myself to him, not that he'd be interested in a 40 year old man with pudgy thighs... pudgy everything, really.

I hadn't "let myself go," it's how I'd always been. Tedd was taller and thinner—and because of the expensive way he dressed always resembled one of the guys in Ralph Lauren ads, like he was going from playing polo to piloting a sleek silver plane.

I was sure Tedd was more Tom's type, but if Tom went for personality, I'd win because I'd had to develop charm and a sense of humor to overcome my pudginess, whereas Tedd was so good looking he didn't need any personality at all. Oddly, that was one of the reasons I thought we had worked as a couple: he looked great around the house, or next to me at the farmer's market, but I never had to worry about him upstaging me creatively.

Wow, that made me sound like a shallow person. I don't think I am. But did shallow people ever think they were? I was a writer; feeling deeply was my job, though sometimes not having to feel was a relief...

Enough of that—We were different and that was good. He made clothes and I made movies. We were "a great couple" especially when he'd make clothes for me and we'd walk side by side, looking like perfect gays in our coordinated but not matching pastel colors and expensively distressed leather shopping bags made to look like they'd been through WWII.

I liked being *that* couple...

I'd loved Tedd since I was 18. We met as seniors in high school, which would make me now... do I have to say it? Yes, Dory tells me I have to say it, that's the point of this whole exercise. OK, fine, I'm 40. Ish. 41, but just barely.

Tedd was the jock and I was the journalist, writing a funny, entirely fictional gossip column for the school paper. He was captain of the swim team (of course) and led them to victory so many times that I wrote a silly column about how he and the "Douglas Dolphins" would save the world. He came over to thank me for making him laugh and I thanked him for thanking me, and we must have been very tired and hot because we fell into my twin bed together, naked.

Even months after we split up, just thinking about him started the waterworks. I thought I was over him, I really did. I was living in our house... *my* house... and he moved in with Jez, can you fucking believe it? I never gave the pink/orange sweater back, but I also couldn't wear it so I gave it to the Goodwill. Somewhere there was a colorful if itchy homeless person.

I tried inviting Martyn over to comfort me with his penis, but he was in Brazil doing a mansion and probably its owner.

Then I tried "dating" apps: *Scruff* and *Growlr*. Dating, my ass. Well, they all wanted my ass but I was never a bottom—and I wanted more than that. I wanted a real boyfriend I could parade around the Silver Lake Farmers Market where I knew Tedd and Jez would be buying kale (now I hate kale more than I ever did), so I could show him, show *them* that I was just fine and my adorable 24-year-old Olympic flamethrower boyfriend thought so, too. I later felt I should get my story straight and discovered, to my chagrin, that flamethrowing was not an Olympic event.

Still, I was pleasantly surprised that even though I had aged out of being a "twink" (young and cute) I was now considered a "daddy" (older... no, *mature* and cute) and there was no end of young men who were interested in me.

Given the fact that I've never looked like a model, except for maybe one in a Build-A-Bear catalog, it still surprised me that *anybody* would find me attractive.

I once saw a neon sign that said "everybody is somebody's reason to masturbate."

Still, wouldn't they rather be with someone young and beautiful like themselves? The answer turned out to be *no*. They were looking for a *daddy*.

LAWRENCE

I didn't have daddy issues, I had a great father who loved me. I'd just always found older men attractive. When I was 8 I had a crush on Bob Hoskins, the actor who played Smee in Peter Pan. He made me feel tingly!

I loved that David was mature. I found mature men better listeners, more intelligent, civilized and sexy. They didn't play relationship games like immature guys my own age—and they were more experienced in the hay too—less rushed, more sensual.

David made me feel *less* disposable—*more* appreciated. He was intelligent, civilized, gentle, and took me seriously. He made me feel the way I wanted to feel about myself.

DAVID

I finally understood the daddy thing. I was a young Santa Claus / Rabbi type, which, to my great surprise and luck, was considered *hot* by certain young gay men. It was hard for me to see myself as desirable, but a friend said, "Don't question it! Let it wash over you, like shampoo." After a while, I stopped doubting it and started accepting it. Why not?

Still, when I thought I might be growing a double-chin, I grew a beard. Then I thought about coloring it because there were too many gray hairs—but that just seemed to make me more attractive to the young'uns.

I had a number of "dates," if you want to call the "I'm tired and hot, let's take off our clothes," meetings "dates." They were fun. Sometimes there'd even be dinner involved— usually me making it or buying it. The trouble with being a daddy was that you're usually expected to pay for things like a real daddy would. I didn't mind that much, but I also didn't want to feel like an ATM with legs.

I tried to avoid looking at Tedd's Instagram which projected an image of, "Envy me, handsome mature model-type man in pants that are too short so you can see my sexy ankles and a jacket that looks too small but was designed that way to show off my defined chest parts..." whatever they're called, I can't remember the word because I never could make mine do anything and I got bored lifting heavy things. Where was I? I felt lost.

Jez's Instagram was filled with pictures of him and Tedd as a "perfect couple." "Here we are in our small but expensive swimsuits!" When not enrobed in a colorful sweater, Jez also had those good chest muscles, *pecs*, that's what they're called. "Look at us, the perfect couple laughing as we get into our Lamborghini!" Or "Vicariously enjoy us, the perfect couple flying business class, toasting champagne glasses and eating caviar!" Yuk.

Or the absolute worst, the one that I took a screenshot of, then instantly wanted to delete but never could, and which Google photos so graciously showed me every couple of weeks in the "Highlights of Tedd" section I never told it to stop showing. It was a picture of the two of them in tight-fitting business suits at the White Fucking House laughing with Kamala. WTF? I mean, seriously, what the fuckity fuck?

If that wasn't bad enough, it made me wonder if *they* were having three-ways with Pete Buttigieg, something that seemed quite natural and nauseating. I had to take a moment— I'd thrown up a little bit in my mouth.

I took 10 cleansing breaths, said my mantra and took a few cannabis mints to get myself back under control.

SHELLI

I said to David, "Maybe Tedd and Jez were meant to be, like Woody and Soon Yi. If that was the case, then gezuntaheit, they should have a lifetime of happiness and, if possible, hemorrhoids." It was lovely to be able to make *him* laugh for a change.

DAVID

Shelli always knew the right thing to make me feel better.

It also felt better to "date" men half my age, though they sometimes made me tired (I'd already taken off my clothes and gone to bed, how much more should I be expected to do?).

What I really wanted to do was *cuddle*. Straight people don't know this about gay people, well, some gay people, a lot of us, is that sex is all fine and good and sometimes we're animals and can't control ourselves (you straight people know what this is like, too, or at least you did before you met your husband or wife). But, mostly, we want to cuddle. And kiss, kissing is important, too. Cuddle and eat popcorn and watch *RuPaul's Drag Race*. Heaven.

Some of the young men who would "date" me would, in fact, like to cuddle. They'd most often want to be the "little spoon," so I could have my big, strong (or at least pudgy, I need a more attractive word for that—*husky?* No, that sounds too much like muscles which I don't have. *Zaftig* is a good word but most people don't know what it means. I don't care, I'm going to use it anyway) arms around them.

That was sweet, like a couple of randy puppies. Sometimes they'd even spend the night. I'd wake up around 4am and peel myself off them, then go to pee. When I came back they'd either be awake and dressed, or they'd turned onto their other side so I was now just sharing my bed with a total stranger, or a semi-stranger whose last name I didn't know.

SHELLI

Then he met Lawrence of Arabia. That's what I called Lawrence. East-Indian and beautiful. Sweet—and so elegant he made Tedd look like a neanderthal.

DAVID

Lawrence was studying geology so that he could join the family business. I even knew Lawrence's last name, Chinnaswami, though I couldn't pronounce it without him giggling. His first name was really *Lufti*, but here he told people to call him Lawrence.

Lufti means "kind and gentle" and he was incredibly kind. He always asked me what I wanted to do. And then he'd do it. He'd take me out to dinner and he'd pay.

When we'd run into someone he knew at, say, Wolfgang Puck's *Spago*, he'd introduce me as his "mentor" and proceed to tell them how wise I was.

In private, he liked how funny I was. I'd written his favorite movie, *Plane Jane*, about a female airline captain of a private luxury jet. It starred Melissa McCarthy, early in her career when nobody knew who she was, as the pilot of a private jet who is picking up 12 orphans, kids of all races aged 2 - 14, from *New Uppsalandia*, a tiny northeastern European monarchy I invented. She's bringing them back to Los Angeles where they'll be adopted by childless movie stars (played by B-level TV personalities, like that actress who was on that thing... I can't remember her name now... nobody can).

But it turns out that the adoption agency didn't get the right papers, and the country's rules are *draconian* (Captain Melissa hears that term and is afraid of vampires, and, it turns out, children). Border patrol won't let the orphans out of the country and if they're not out in three days their adoptions expire! (That's not how it actually works, but nobody ever complained except an adoption worker in Spokane and nobody read her blog, except me).

So Captain Melissa must adopt all 12 orphans herself! The eldest, Sophie, knowing Melissa's fear of vampires, claims to be one, even going so far as to bite her neck. Just imagine an 18 hour flight with 12 kids screaming, "Are we there yet" (at first in an unknown language, but learning the phrase in English as the story progresses), a failing jet engine, a possible crash landing, then Captain Melissa saving the day— and deciding to keep all 12 kids (much to the chagrin of that actress from that show I can't remember).

Basically hilarity ensues, followed by tears.

Lawrence said he'd seen the movie 27 times when he was growing up as it was the only movie his nanny could find that had *no* profanities or nudity or smoking. I wrote it when I was 27 for a producer, Marc Gold of "GoldMark" productions. He wanted a movie with no profanities or nudity or smoking so it could sell to mothers who were concerned about such things. We got a gold seal of approval from *Mothers for Pure Children*, a group that Marc created himself.

The movie was a sleeper hit. It cost almost nothing to make and earned over $100 million, which launched my writing career as the king of "Clean Comedies," movies without swearing or sex. That was fine with me, until a friend from the USC writing program I'd been in got an Oscar for writing edgy films explicitly about swearing and sex.

My former-friend-the-Oscar winner was one J. Michael Connasse, who I'd never liked because he was a plagiarist. In class he presented a scene straight out of a Woody Allen movie. I don't mean inspired by, I mean the same scene. It was the one from *Take the Money and Run* where Woody tries to hold up a cashier and his handwriting is so bad she thinks he's written, "I have a gub." That scene. Verbatim.

The teacher had never seen the movie and went on and on about how brilliant J. Michael was. From that day forward I never trusted anyone with the first initial "J" that I assumed meant, "Jackass."

Now this Jackass "wrote" *Wet Wednesday,* which I knew to be a copy of a Japanese gay porn (don't ask how I knew this). The original porn was dark, dangerous and divine. Few people outside of Japan had ever seen it but I was in Tokyo for the opening of one of my clean comedies, *Bark Buddies,* a comedy about a pair of mutant police dogs who have to save the world from the same nuclear waste that turned them into mutants. It was a huge hit in Japan, second only to *The Matrix*, which in Japan and Latvia, *Bark Buddies* outsold on DVD.

Wet Wednesday was a bad copy of *Bukkake Nichiyōbi* (a polite translation would be *Very Wet Sunday*). Still, Jackass' copy was shocking enough that the MPAA almost gave it an X. At least that was the story put out to the media for publicity. The truth was the producers purposely put in some explicit shots to get it an X rating, then agreed to remove them to get an R.

And what did all this buzz get? An Oscar for best screenplay! I could have written a more emotionally rich film out of the source material I'd seen many, many times. But Jackass just focused on the sex. He only added one new scene—at a Macodonaldo's (McDonald's) that was disturbing in so many ways.

I even admitted to Dory that I was jealous. But more than that, I was angry that this Jackass was getting feted when he was merely fetid.

Still, Lawrence loved *Plain Jane* and by extension, me, and that was some consolation, especially when I bought him a metallic gold speedo and had him pose like an Oscar.

He even went with me to the Farmer's Market so we could smile and laugh and touch each other's arms while ancient Tedd and elderly Jez looked on.

It didn't make me feel better.

What did, was when Lawrence said, "I want to be your real boyfriend."

Well, it did for a moment until I started to wonder how that was going to work. I wasn't literally old enough to be his father... oh, wait... I'd experimented with a girl when I was 15. If she'd gotten pregnant, and lived in Mumbai, I *would* be old enough to be his father!

While I'd already introduced him to a few of my friends, (Shelli said, "What a delicious little morsel he is!"), what if he introduced me to his friends and they said something like, "It's nice you brought your dad along"? Then what?

I brought this up with him, and he said, "I expect they would say 'Lawrence, how did you land such a handsome and talented man?'"

Again, very sweet, but I didn't believe it. And what about his parents? I couldn't imagine his father would accept that his young son's boyfriend was his own age!

It was impossible.

LAWRENCE

First, I was 28. I don't know why David thought I was 24. I also don't know why he was so bad at maths. He was not old enough to be my father. And I was mature enough to know I was not his first just as he knew that he was not my first. Despite what I told him, he refused to believe me when I said he was cuter than my ex-boyfriend, Anderson Cooper.

Next, my father, Bashir, was 50 years old—actually old enough to be my father. He knew I was gay since I was 4 years old and I would wear my mother's jewels and shoes. Father's own identical twin brother, Fareed, was gay, "the pink sheep of the family." His family dealt with it by setting him up with his own fashion house, *Fari*, in far away Milan. He and my father were always very close. In fact, my uncle introduced my father to my mother, Laila.

LAILA

My dear sweet boy, Lufti. So pretty. So gentle. So artistic. So gay. It ran in Bashir's family, and honestly, given Bashir's taste in gaudy rings I sometimes even wondered about him, too.

BASHIR

There was clearly something wrong with Laila's genes for Lufti to turn out the way he was. But he was a sweet boy, a good boy, a gay boy. Still, I held out hope he would marry a nice girl, but I wasn't holding my breath.

LAWRENCE

I was raised to listen and bow to the will of my parents. To be a good son. Obedient. Agreeable. Compliant. Thankfully, while I was studying geology, it was acceptable for me to study my real passion, gemology, because I could be a jewelry designer for my uncle's Fareed's company.

David was correct when he said that I said I wanted him to be my boyfriend. I did. I liked that he was mature (not old, though he thought he was old which could get tiresome). My friends already thought he was a catch because he wrote movies, and, like me, they all grew up with Plain Jane. My straight friend, Reza, married a woman who looked a lot like Melissa McCarthy, as well as naming his Gulfstream jet Plain Jane. That should tell you.

I met David at Shelli's holiday party. Shelli is Jewish, like David, so it wasn't a Christmas party, though she had a 25 foot Christmas tree made out of chrome car bumpers with crash dummy heads as ornaments. Shelli had a tremendous art collection, which is why I was there, because my best friend since university, Yasmin, worked for Hauser & Wirth and sold Shelli the piece, titled, "Tree of Death," by "the artist known as Andre Andre XIV."

Shelli's house was very modern, all glass walls and reflecting pools. I caught David's eye through one of these big glass walls. I almost stepped into the reflecting pool to get a closer look but Yasmin caught me just in time. David walked towards me and ran into the glass, falling backwards and luckily landing on a Claus Oldenburg soft sculpture of a clothespin.

I ran inside to make sure he was OK. When he regained consciousness he looked at me and simply said, "you." That's when I knew it wasn't an accident we had met. I'd had a dream three or four months earlier where I saw myself in a mirror and when I woke up, I was someone else who looked at me and said, "you," so I knew this was predestined.

Later David asked me what I saw in him. I said, "It was like that glass window was a mirror, and I was seeing my future self." He joked, "Like in 20 years," and I said, "You don't look a day over 40," and he said "That's because I am 40," but really he was 41, so my compliment was a good one!

I have tried to explain to him how seeing a future reflection of myself was a mystical thing—that we had a cosmic connection. But he usually made a joke about how he was "so big he could be seen from space," which is funny but not true. He was not nearly that big. And he did not believe me when I said I liked the way he's big. And no, not in the dirty way, where he is not big. He tells me not to say that but it is true and I like it and that's that.

Yasmin will tell you that once I met David, I was always saying, "David said the funniest thing..." or "David made the most delicious tempura Parmesan," or "David makes me feel beautiful." Despite how David described me, I never felt like a handsome man. My nose was large and my eyebrows could be seen from space! See what I did there? I was learning from David.

Honestly, my eyebrows were so big that when I was a teenager I would go to my sister's eyebrow threader, Maha. Her name meant "wild cow" and she was a cow of a woman, but very talented with the threads. She made my eyebrows smaller and shaped like Elizabeth Taylor's.

But Anderson convinced me to let them grow out, so I did. He said, "Lulu, (that's what he called me), this is your face, own it." So I did, only occasionally plucking a long stray hair that would seemingly grow overnight.

I was glad I didn't have a unibrow, no, it was two separate eyebrows, though they were so long they almost went to my ears. I learned to own it, but I didn't like it until I met David. He would stroke my eyebrows in a way that made me shiver. He told me I looked like an ancient God. At first I laughed, thinking he was once again being funny, but he meant it—and when he stroked my eyebrows, I could close my eyes, relax, and unfurrow my brow.

I was a worrier by nature. "What if there is an earthquake?" "What if my parents are lost at sea?" "What if my DVD drive breaks and I can't find a copy of *Plane Jane?*"

But David stroked my eyebrows and said, "Most things we worry about never happen." I remembered that none of those things had happened, or were likely to happen and *Plane Jane* was available streaming.

David was very wise as well as funny. He was also crazy but not in such a bad way. I believe it was Tedd who made him crazy. I did not like Tedd or that Jez person. They both must be stupid to have let David go, but I am lucky they did. I made sure that Shelli posted a picture of David and me on her Instagram for Tez (what I call Tedd and Jez) to see. I was wearing the gold speedo David gave me and he was wearing a tuxedo, holding me as if he'd just won an Oscar. He won something better— me.

I am not a writer like David, but I could design beautiful necklaces and he couldn't :) I designed him a boyfriend ring I was wearing on a chain around my neck, but I hadn't shown it to him yet as I wanted it to be a surprise.

DAVID

Lu (his ex, Anderson, called him *Lulu* but I thought 'Lu' was cuter) wouldn't let me read what he wrote. He said he's not a writer and it's not very good. I said, "but you can design beautiful necklaces and I can't." He really does design beautiful jewelry. His drawings are so artistic by themselves that Shelli insisted on buying eight to frame and fill a wall of her dressing room which is bigger than my house. OK, that's an exaggeration, it's bigger than my house, excluding the garage.

When I met him, it was like that song, *Some Enchanted Evening*, I saw him across a crowded room. Except I saw him through a window and ran into it and passed out. That should have been embarrassing enough to put him off, but he was there when I regained consciousness and said he'd dreamed about me.

Even with my crashing headache I thought, "This is too much like a Nancy Meyers movie so I have clearly died and gone to her version of heaven." This was confirmed when the waiter brought around trays of tiny bacon wrapped scallops and Lu grabbed the entire tray and fed them to me one by one. An entire tray of hors d'oeuvres? He couldn't have known these were my favorite, but he did. He claimed this was another sign we were meant to meet, and to me it was another sign that I was actually dead. But somewhere in my youth and childhood, I must have done something good, because this is where I ended up.

He drove me home and put me to bed— *cuddling* with me all night. Even after I came back from the bathroom.

It was hard not to love this man, but I was on the rebound and clearly not thinking straight, so it didn't seem like a good idea.

All I could do was think of our differences. He was young and God-like. I was old and had too, too much mortal flesh. I was Jewish. He was Hindu. My parents would *shtarbn* (die) and his would *hatya* (kill me).

Yes, he told me about his father and his uncle and how they wouldn't mind, but I couldn't imagine them being pleased to imagine him in bed with an old... mature Jew.

He stayed that first night and basically never left. I'd come home and he'd be there, reorganizing my drawers to make room for more of his clothes.

I was so happy.

LAWRENCE

I was so happy.

DAVID

I was so happy I couldn't write. My brain was cool, calm, quiet. All the buzzing and noise was gone, replaced with the feeling of a warm, sandy beach where I only wanted to bask in Lu's presence. Days went by. No words came out of my head.

It was bliss. It was terrible.

Terrible got me thinking.

I wasn't even officially divorced from Tedd, who, having heard through the grapevine (and my Instagram) that I was with someone, appeared at the door, wearing one of Jez's eye-searingly bright sweaters.

"Can I come in and talk?" he asked innocently.

"Does Hitler poop in the woods?" I shot back at him.

"I'm not Hitler, Davey."

"In that sweater there's a strong resemblance."

He laughed. He always laughed at my jokes. I loved that about him. *Loved*, past tense. Now it irritated me. He must have wanted something.

"What do you want," I said, not letting him in.

"To congratulate you on your new boyfriend," he smiled with too many, too-white teeth.

"Have you whitened your teeth or did you swallow a set of mahjong tiles?" I said through my frozen smile, knowing it was a stupid thing to say.

"I thought I should bring this personally," he said, holding a blue leather Tiffany box containing his wedding ring.

I stopped breathing for a few seconds. Who does that? I mean, really, who does that? I wasn't wearing my ring but I also wasn't going to sell it to "Cash4Gold." It represented too many years of my life to simply get rid of. Yet there he was, handing me his like it meant nothing to him.

"You always had fat fingers," I said, not wanting to touch the ring as if it was "my precious," and I'd turn into Gollum.

He handed me an envelope, "Sign these and we can both move on," he said, smiling again. I wanted to knock his teeth over like bowling pins, but I never had much upper body strength.

I heard a horn honking. Oh, how nice, Jez was waiting for him in a Lamborghini. "I wish you much happiness with your new boyfriend," he said.

I thought, "I hope your ugly yellow car careens off Mulholland Drive," but actually said, "Um. You, two." Yes, I actually thought of "two" rather than "too" because I was stunned by those two. Once it came out of my mouth I was pretty sure he took it as "too," like "also," because he smiled again, and I didn't bother to correct him because it was pointless not to mention churlish.

He walked away with his perky ass and jumped in the car with Jez who had the audacity to wave and burn rubber at the same time. Fuck them both.

The weird thing is, I didn't hate them as much as I thought I should. They were like two vacuous vacuformed Ken dolls. They deserved each other.

But did I deserve Lu? Was he going to wake up one morning, look over at my drooling face, the veil being lifted from his beautiful gray eyes and run screaming from my life? It felt like it was only a matter of time, as it had been with Tedd.

I didn't have time to ruminate on that today. Lu was off at UCLA to study one kind of rock or another, and I had a deadline on revisions for my latest clean comedy, *Doctor What?,* about a Black shoe-shine boy who, though a series of fortunate events, becomes Hollywood's podiatrist to the stars, Dr. Sherman Wexler. It was based on a true story I knew would interest Marc Gold because he had a foot fetish. Plus, feet were deemed clean body parts by the MPCC, an organization Marc created.

But now I wanted to write a movie with sex and swearing! Naked sweaty bodies cursing while fucking! Oscar bait!

I went through Marc's notes and made all his requested changes without even protesting. My heart wasn't in it. Did I care if the shoes were oxfords or wingtips? No. Did I care if they were cordovan instead of brown? Fuck no! Did I care that the boy I'd written as mixed race be changed to blond... OK, that I cared about. I didn't change it and wouldn't mention it before I sent the script to casting.

No— I was thinking about my dream project, *Stunning Aliens.* I had it mapped out in my head, even if I hadn't yet written a word. The aliens, Zorn and Norz, couldn't be nicer, smarter, or sexier. Think young Brad Pitt and young Salma Hayak. Think of them naked. Glistening. Because their skin just naturally glistened. And no, I didn't get that from the stupid sparkly vampires in *Twilight,* I got that from the way Tedd looked when... oh, never mind.

Anyway, the aliens come to Earth to teach us the secret to peace and prosperity — sex!

Unfortunately their beauty, goodness and unearthly spectacular Instagram account causes humans to become insanely jealous! Humans hate them and want to fuck them, both, sometimes at the same time! Zorn and Norz know how to help humans live in peace and love, but can humanity live with the idea that there's an alien race much better than all of us?

I couldn't wait to write this black comedy, one in which, from the Alien POV, humans are the monsters (Tedd inspired that part, too).

I sat looking at the screen and all I could think of was Lu's face. So beautiful he could be an alien. But he was also human, and he wasn't a monster, so as lovely as that was, it undermined my desire to write.

I wrote best when I was unhappy. Then writing was an escape. But now Lu was making me happy and it was undermining my work and was making me cranky.

DORY

Confidential notes for my eyes only: At least twice a month I have to tell David, "Have you ever had a problem writing before? No! So you have factual proof that it won't happen now." He doesn't listen. He's a nudnik.

I know I asked for this job, but I'm human, I still get annoyed, and when he tells me crap like, "I can only write when I'm unhappy," I mention many famous writers who were happy. Yes, they were also on amphetamines, but that was beside the point.

OK, so his mother was bipolar and his father was distant. I was trying to get him to focus on why his love of writing somehow negated his own desire to be loved.

David was clearly crazy about Lawrence... not crazy crazy, which isn't a technical term or diagnoses, I meant it in the colloquial sense. Yet David wanted to keep him at a distance. Obviously it was a direct causal effect from the trauma he experienced with Tedd, the twat.

I tried to report Jez to the Mental Institute of National Directors, MIND, but he wasn't listed. I tried the California Regional Association of Professionals, but he wasn't there either. I did a Google search and his website lists him, and I quote, as a "Couples and Sexy Therapist" with offices in Beverly Hills and "Jackson's Hole." I did not make that up. He has a bunch of random letters after his name that have absolutely no credibility to anyone with a brain, which is how I know Tedd must have chosen him.

TEDD

Jez constantly impressed me with his cred.

And his abs.

LAWRENCE

You know how you can just smell a problem? It's not an actual smell in your nose, it's this sense, maybe a spidey-sense. I'm not very good at explaining this stuff but I need to write this down otherwise I worry about it.

Dory, who's Dave's therapist, is now also my therapist. He recommended her because he said she'd helped him so much, and I liked that she knew David well enough so that if I ran into something she'd have sound advice. I assumed she'd heard a lot about me, too, hopefully all good.

I told her about this smell, and she said, "You need to talk to him about it. When these things rattle around in your head they take on a life of their own that doesn't match that of the outside world." That made a lot of sense.

When I got home I said, "David, we need to talk," and he got this look on his face like I'd slapped him or was going to slap him. He cringed. I worried.

"You're worried, I can see it." He said, looking worried himself. "Did I do something wrong? Did you find someone better? Are you leaving me?" I heard the sad little boy in his voice.

"No, nothing like that. I'm sorry. Dory didn't tell me you'd be so upset when she told me to talk to you."

"Dory is telling you about me?"

"No, she told *me* to talk to *you*."

"Oh, shit, I knew this day was coming. You're too good to be true."

"No, stop," I tell him, touching his cheek, then stroking his eyebrow like he did to me. He shook his head and rubbed it like I'd made it itch. "She told me to talk to you because I sensed something's wrong with *you*."

"*Me?* Wrong? Like I'm dying wrong?" He was starting to sweat.

I took his hand. "Let's start over, David, OK? You didn't do anything wrong. I'm not leaving." I felt his hand relax. "Tell me what's going on inside that sexy brain of yours, OK?"

He looked around the room, anywhere but at me. I put my hand on his tummy, a reminder to take slow, cleansing breaths like Dory had taught us both.

He finally said, "I'm too happy."

"And that's a problem, why?"

"This isn't your fault. I mean, it's my fault, it's my problem, it's me being me. The whole time with Tedd I thought I was happy because I looked happy..."

He went on and on and didn't make a lot of sense to me. I'm glad Dory could make sense of him.

DORY

Confidential: David didn't make sense. Lawrence was a catch. Handsome. Smart, getting his doctorate. If he wasn't gay and my daughter wasn't a lesbian I would set them up.

But, given the situation, I wondered if he and David were a good match. That's not for me to decide, but I suggested to Lawrence that he make a list of his priorities because we can so easily get distracted.

He said, "Love is my number one priority."

I asked him if he was putting David's needs before his own.

He said, "David's what I need."

I asked him to consider his studies and own personal creative goals, but he was fixated on making David happy.

Why could I never meet a man like this? Was it because they're all gay? I was beginning to think my daughter had the right idea.

DAVID

When I was with Tedd I thought I was happy because I *looked* happy. Everything in my life looked perfect, right? So it must have been right and that marshmallowy feeling I had of inferiority was just how life felt, right? I figured I just hadn't learned how to live life the right way—like Tedd had.

That's why I started to see Dory. Tedd didn't need a therapist because he had a haberdasher. And because he wasn't that bright.

Lu was bright, but I clearly hadn't explained myself well enough because he rambled, "So what you're saying is... I don't know what you're saying."

"I'm *trying* to say that I now realize I was never totally happy with Tedd and that made me more creative. You've shown me what true happiness is."

Then I could almost see the cartoon light bulb go off above Lu's head. "And that's bad? Yes, that's bad because I've made you uncreative."

"No, no, *you* haven't made me uncreative. I've made myself, no, see..."

"I don't see how this isn't my fault." Lu said, matter-of-factly.

"It's not your fault that you make me happy!" I stated, starting to get frustrated with myself for not being able to explain it clearly. This was when I was better in writing, where I could put it on paper and edit it until it was right. Talking was harder because once I said something, it was said and there was no taking it back. I mean, you could try but it was messy and never quite forgotten. Like the times when Tedd would suggest I might want to drop a few pounds, then would backpedal and say, "you're not *that* fat," which did not help at all.

"Look, Lu, I love you." I told him this every day, so it wasn't like a movie moment where the music swells and you hold your breath to see if the other person says it, too. But this time I did hold my breath.

"I love you, too, David. I want you to be happy, but you seem to be happy and unhappy at the same time. I want you to be more happy than unhappy. So what do you want me to do?"

His asking me this caused a warm wave of love to wash over me. Then I felt a sharp twinge of self-loathing run down my spine. I loved him for being so sweet and hated myself for being so crazy.

The writer in me finally kicked in. I hated stories where a character's problems got worse because they wouldn't just come out and say it— so I was going to come out and say it.

"I can't write when you're around. This is my problem. This is my fault. The other thing is that I still think about Tedd a lot. Not in a good way. I wouldn't take him back if he came to the door wearing a grass skirt and singing 'Bali Hai.'"

"Do you want me to wear a grass skirt and sing? You know I can't sing." Lu explained, sincerely.

"But you have beautiful legs. No, sorry, I don't want you to do that. Actually, I do want you to do that but it's not what I'm talking about now. I need some space between Tedd and you. I have to get him out of my mind. He's the mean voice in my head and I don't want him saying anything bad about you." I thought for a moment, "When there's nothing bad about you."

Lu sat there for a while, looking at his hands. He had beautiful hands, smooth olive skin, long fingers, and flat nails. I liked the way they looked and felt and he moved them gracefully. He folded them in his lap, looked me in the eyes and said, "So you want me to leave."

"No!" I almost yelled, and Lu stood up. "No, sorry, please, no. I know I'm being stupid but I just need a little time and space, OK? Just a little. I'd like us to spend weekends together. Then I can write during the week. I'll keep talking to Dory about this and I'll get over it, but that's what I'd like for now."

Lu sat down and calmly said, "You want me to be your weekend boyfriend. Does this mean you'll have a different boyfriend during the week?"

"No, please, Lu. Oh fuck, this seemed simpler in my head. No, I'm not going to see anyone else. If you want to see someone else then you should see someone else."

He looked down at his hands again. "You asshole." Then he stood up and walked to the front door. I sat there, frozen until my writerly brain kicked in, seeing the scenario of letting him leave because I was too crazy or stupid or proud to stop him. In this case, I was too crazy and stupid and lacking in pride to let him go.

I threw myself in front of the door with my arms out blocking the way. "I'm an asshole who loves you."

"I thought people were supposed to get more mature as they got older," he said, not in a mean way.

"We are. I am. I will. Being more mature means you can also get more screwed up. Please just give me some time, OK? It'll give you time, too, because I don't want you to be stuck with my craziness if you don't want to be."

"I want you to *not* be crazy," he said in a very non-crazy way.

"I want that, too. I'm working on it." I put my arms around him. He felt stiff at first, but then relaxed and put his hands around me. I felt his stomach expanding and contracting against me as he took his own deep breaths.

He let go of me and put his hands on my shoulders. "OK, it's Tuesday so I'm going back to my apartment until Saturday..."

"Friday night," I interrupted.

"Until Friday night. This might be good for me, too, I have a lot of work to do on my thesis and I haven't been doing it here."

"See? Good!" I said cheerfully. He stared at me, eyebrows raised, then exhaled, kissed me and left.

The click of the door latch made me instantly sad and miserable. I was ready to write!

DORY

Confidential: After listening to David for an hour I wanted to shake him. Or call his friend Shelli and have her shake him, as that seemed like something she'd do. She sounded fun, I would have liked to meet her, but of course I couldn't. That was definitely one of the downsides of this job.

SHELLI

I was delighted my David was finally rid of Tedd and had that talented little tidbit, Lawrence. Very happy for him.

Life is short. Love should be long, though my favorite husbands had a bad habit of dying and my worst husband, Syd, refused to die, even after we'd drunk way too much 1959 Dom Perignon and I tried to strangle him with his own Turnbull and Asser necktie.

He thought it was auto-erotic asphyxiation and had such an intense *la petite mort* I was sure he was dead. He wasn't. Even divorce didn't kill him, though signing his settlement check almost killed me.

LAWRENCE

My first boyfriend was Ian, my roommate at Oxford. He was pale and blond and as different from me as he could possibly be. His parents owned a chain of tyre stores called "Blondie's" because they were all towheads.

He was short and skinny and very pretty, but also bony. Sometimes when we had sex his bones would jab into me painfully. Cuddling him was like trying to cuddle a skeleton. Still, I was fascinated by him: so English, so refined, with a very posh accent I wanted to emulate.

Early on Ian said to me, "I like you because my parents will hate you." I laughed, because my parents would have hated him, too. They were snobs about snobs.

Easter break we went to his family's big house in the country. It was a new house that tried to look like a castle. Fake stone, shiny marble. Grotesque in both meanings of the word.

His parents were nice to me in that way people are when they can't stand you. That's when I realized Ian had told me the truth, and I remembered a quote I once read, "When someone tells you who they are, believe them."

I took long walks alone and cried. I felt stupid, and angry. When I got back to school I asked to be transferred to another room. When the housing manager asked me why, I said, "because Ian's cruel."

I knew David wasn't cruel. Just neurotic in the way Jewish comedians talk about being. He said so, somewhat often, "Ugh, I'm so crazy," or "Don't mind me, I'm crazy," or "our problems don't amount to a hill of beans in this crazy world," which I recognized as having been said by Humphrey Bogart in *Casablanca* and was probably not the best example.

So David was crazy. He came out and told me so. I figured it was "cute crazy" like in the movies.

I could deal with crazy. I wasn't good with cruel—Tedd was cruel—in that Ian way. Just as it took me a long time to get over how Ian treated me, I understood it was going to take David a while, too.

When I told Yasmin about this, she said, "You're the perfect boyfriend, Boo! Why do you have to be so gay?"

"You're the perfect girlfriend," I replied. "Why do you have to be a girl?"

Then we kissed and hugged and drank wine and watched "Enchanted April," because it always made us feel warm and summery.

Wednesday was busy with classes. Thursday was a half-day, the other half was spent working on my thesis and looking at photos of David, wishing I could have his baby. I was too embarrassed to tell Dory about it until we got into a discussion about kids and I mentioned it. She's so nice and said, "That's a natural creative impulse."

Still, it felt weird. I have cis male friends who want to be girls and that's fine but that wasn't what I wanted. Once after we made love I said to David, "I wish I could have your baby." It just came out before I could censor myself. He held my face in his hands, kissed me and said, "I wish you could, too." We didn't say any more than this and it felt right in the moment.

When I was a little kid I thought women had babies in the toilet—they came out like poop. That's what I thought for the longest time, so as a kid I thought I could have a baby, too. I checked the toilet each time I pooped in case there was a baby because I didn't want it to drown. It's embarrassing even to remember this, but I was just a kid.

I'm not a kid anymore and thinking about it made me uncomfortable, so I went back to work on my thesis which distracted me.

Thursday felt very long. I didn't call David, but I did send him two text messages. One said, "I just had two impossible burger tacos," and the next said, "Can we bake bread this weekend?"

He sent me three text messages, "Yummy!" and "Of course!" Then Friday at 11:14 a.m. he sent one that said, "I miss you and can't wait to see you." That made me very happy. I took a screenshot of it.

DAVID

I finished an entire clean comedy in a week...

J. MICHAEL

I've heard some guys take an entire week to write a script. I can copy and paste one in 20 minutes. No, wait, I have to do a search and replace for the names. It's also a good idea to translate some of the dialog to Klingon or another made-up language. Seems more exotic and dramatic, can't be traced, and subtitles are expected to be stilted which plays to my style. With all that to contend with, I generally give it a day, including a lunch break and time spent watching porn.

DAVID

...In it, Claire, the 16-year-old daughter of a single female pharmacist, invents a new drug called *Joyex* that makes people happy. It's entirely organic, made from dandelions and turmeric and has no side effects. It's so effective that it's immediately banned by the government after much lobbying from so-called conservative business owners who claim people will stop coming to work. Claire and her mother create an underground network to spread the recipe, leading to a big musical number where everyone sings in perfect harmony, like that old Coke commercial.

MARC

I texted David, "What the fuck are you thinking? Are you trying to fucking ruin me? We can't promote drug taking you shithead! Change the drug to a dog, and make the girl find the perfect puppies for people to make them happy. We can get product placement from Purina and the whole thing pays for itself. Have it back on my desk in a week."

DAVID

I snoozed the email till Monday. I could make the revision in two days, then have three to work on my *Stunning Aliens*! I'd talk to my agent and start taking meetings and get it sold and get an Oscar for something *original*, not like J. Asshole Whatever.

I was already happy by the time I heard Lu's key in the lock. Knowing his love of tacos and the fact that we couldn't be together on Tuesdays, I made "International Tacos" using fake chicken (he was too sweet to eat animals) and three different sauces, mole, pomodoro, and stroganoff. I had corn tortillas, lavash and focaccia.

His face lit up when he came in the door. "What are those incredible smells?"

I was excited and wanted to tell him but first I had to hug him and kiss him and knowing this could happen, had prepared everything so it could wait an hour... or two... while we got reacquainted.

I thought I knew every inch of his taut yet soft body, but tonight it all felt new again as I licked him up and down. He tasted salty and sweet. He gasped when I licked the back of his knees and moaned when I took his cock into my mouth. I loved the way he felt and tasted, like the best thing I could ever put in my mouth.

I ran my beard across his beautiful bottom. Tedd's ass was hard, built from endless squats to look good in a pair of slacks. Lu's ass was natural, round and slightly soft. I literally liked to kiss his ass, then rub my beard against it and feel him squirm.

I wanted to make him happy. That took my mind off myself and what he might be thinking about me as it was still light outside which meant there was no hiding my gelatinous parts. He didn't seem to notice them, or, if he did, he didn't mind them the way I did.

We fit together. As I entered him we felt connected like there was nothing between us. I stopped thinking and felt at one with the universe, though I didn't say that. I just said, "I love you."

LAWRENCE

When he was inside me I felt one with him and the universe. I didn't tell him that. I just said, "I love you."

DAVID

I loved the afterglow, too. We held each other and talked about our week. We had so much to share. He told me about his progress on the dissertation— how he'd combined geology and gemology because they were both about rocks. I marveled at this creature next to me— at once so human, and also a beautiful alien. How inspiring!

LAWRENCE

I felt seen by him. He listened to me rattle on about the geological forces of time and pressure necessary to create a gemstone, and his eyes never glazed over when I compared synthetic gems to artificial meat and how they were better for the planet.

He told me about his herb drug story and how his boss wanted him to change it and he didn't mind. This impressed me, because I would have minded.

Then he told me I was an alien. I told him I had to pee and went to the bathroom and looked at myself in the mirror. Was I really that strange? My eyes were widely set under my endless eyebrows. Alien, I could see it. Then I remembered he'd said, *beautiful* alien. I looked in the mirror again. I didn't see the beautiful part myself.

I went back to bed and said, "Squeak, squawk, beep, bop, buzz," the way I thought an alien would. He laughed and kissed me.

DAVID

He didn't know how beautiful he was.

We ate tacos on the patio, the colorful outdoor lighting making him glow green— like the aliens.

He got some stroganoff sauce on his cheek and I licked it off.

We snuggled on an outdoor chaise, covered with a faux fur throw I bought because I thought it would be hot to make love on it in front of the fireplace. We hadn't done that yet. I hoped we would this weekend.

Then we made bread because that's what he wanted to do. Cinnamon raisin bread. It was delicious. He only ate one slice so it was left for me to eat the rest. I mean, I didn't want to hurt his feelings!

LAWRENCE

Monday morning was hard. I didn't want to leave. I put on a brave face, thanked him for a memorable weekend and walked to my car without turning around to look at him. I was sorry I hadn't taken any selfies of us this weekend that I could look at through the week. I would make sure to do that next week.

I let myself be consumed by classes and my dissertation, and going out dancing with Yasmin, Bruno, Cheyenne, and Cubby. Yasmin and Bruno were a thing now, which made her happy, but I didn't like him. Bruno was tall and tough-looking. She told me he looked like Stallone but I thought he just looked like his nose had been broken.

Cheyenne was a cute boy from Wyoming, hence his name. He wore cowboy hats and belt buckles and boots and all that. It wasn't an affectation, it was who he really was. He talked very quietly, so I had to lean in close to hear him, then I'd smell the Doublemint gum he chewed to cover up his chewing tobacco habit. He would have benefited from washing his hair more often because he had dandruff that I was always brushing off him.

Cubby was non-binary. They were short and round and cute in their own way, like a life-size teddy bear. They were studying fashion design and always wore the most interesting getups. Today it was a short red sweater exposing their adorable belly button over a metallic gold pleated skirt with Doc Marten boots. They wore a necklace of shiny red crystals as a kind of headdress. I appreciated their originality and was inspired to design a necklace that could double as a headband/tiara.

We danced and drank and sang karaoke, which I tried to avoid because I can't sing. Cubby said they'd sing with me and we did a duet of "I've got you Babe" where Cubby was both Sonny and Cher and I mostly danced backup.

I texted David a photo of Yasmin, Cheyenne, Cubby and myself while Bruno was in the bathroom for a very long time. I think he was doing coke because he came back with a lot of energy and danced like he thought he was Travolta in Saturday Night Fever. The dance floor cleared for him—not because he was good—but because the other dancers were afraid he was going to kick them.

DORY

Confidential: Even when Lawrence is pining he's cute— the kind of cute where I'd like to have a life-size cutout of him in the corner of my kitchen. I'd see his smile and imagine him saying, "Morning, Dor!" It's not at all romantic, I just like the way he smells.

I suggested that he's young and needs to live his own life rather than waiting around for David.

DAVID

Lu texted me a picture of himself and his friends at a club. Friend his own age. I hate clubs like that—the loud music hurts my ears. My God, I sound like I'm a hundred. I was glad he was enjoying himself. I replied with one of those stupid sticker things of a cartoon character who looked vaguely like me (meaning slightly inflated and wearing round glasses) disco dancing like that Saturday Night Fever actor... I can't remember his name... He was in *Welcome Back Kotter,* and *Grease...*

I didn't leave the house. I worked on the rewrites. Marc had a point about puppies. I added a scene with a dozen puppies piling on Claire that was cute and would get a lot of dogs adopted.

I ate popcorn for dinner. I didn't feel like cooking for myself. That made me sad, and even more productive. I wrote till 3am.

LAWRENCE

Cheyenne kissed me. I knew he had a crush on me but I was surprised when he leaned in and planted one on my lips. I wasn't a fan of the tobacco taste, but his lips were nice and he's a very sweet boy. I closed my eyes and pretended I was a cowboy, too, and we'd been wrangling then doggies or whatever they call it. It was fun.

I liked kissing boys and it wasn't cheating or anything. I didn't think oral was cheating either— it was basically a gay handshake. Besides, did David seriously expect me to go for five entire days without release? He couldn't possibly.

Cheyenne was especially good with his tongue, he ran it flat, up and down my cock, panting like a dog. For a second, his blond hair and blue eyes reminded me of Ian, but Ian was never this generous, and if I blurred my eyes a little bit, Cheyenne looked like a young Robert Redford or Brad Pitt. I had a thing for Brad Pitt who got even more handsome as he got older. That was another conversion I needed to have with David. If I ever meet Brad Pitt he could fuck me. I didn't think there was a high-probability of 1) meeting him, or 2) him wanting to fuck me because he seemed straight, but one must always leave one's options open.

Unlike David's, Cheyenne's cock was very big. I never knew what to do with all that, there's only so much you can fit in your mouth. So I emulated his dog-lick style, which he loved, even so far as making little yapping noises. I wondered if he was one of those guys who has a leather puppy mask at home. No judgment from me, but I never understood that or was the least bit interested in cross-species sex.

David told me about a scene he wanted to write for his alien movie, where they're mating with humans and it's so mind-boggling that the humans literally go insane (their minds having been thoroughly boggled). I didn't know how I felt about this. Humans could do anything they wanted with another consenting human, I was totally fine with that. But, again, the cross-species thing didn't do it for me.

Since David called me an alien I guessed it was one of his fantasies. I didn't mind indulging in that—role-play was fun. I used to like to "conquer" pasty little English schoolmates as an imagined retribution for what they did to my people. Everybody got what they wanted.

But I preferred it when David conquered me. I liked him to be in control.

Right now Cheyenne was losing control in the front seat of my electric Mustang. I'd ordered the leather upholstery for just such a contingency because I didn't want to worry about staining. This was another thing I had in common with David.

DAVID

When I watched porn I worried about the furniture. It was very distracting. If guys were fucking on a fabric sofa (in what I assumed to be a rented house, or probably even just an Airbnb),

I'd obsess about whether or not the sofa had been Scotchguarded. Couldn't they at least have put down a colorful Turkish towel or something? Better yet—rented a place with a leather sofa they could easily wipe off?

When I'd see thumbnails on xTube that showed a fabric sofa I moved right along, knowing I wouldn't be able to focus while worrying about the upholstery.

I remembered how relieved Lu was when he saw I had a leather sofa. Even though he didn't eat animals, he didn't mind that my sofa was made out of one. That was very open-minded of him.

I felt bad making him wait five days before having sex. He was only 28 (he had reminded me I'd been wrong when I thought he was 24), and he needed it at least once, if not twice a day. As an old man of 40 I only needed it once every day... or every two days. Or twice over the weekend, then a visit or two to XTube during the week.

I wanted to talk to Lu about this so there was no confusion. I wouldn't mind if he played around with other guys, especially guys his own age. I'd even find it hot if he told me the details. I just didn't want him playing with guys my age who he might prefer. No, in fact, I didn't want him fooling around with anyone he might prefer to me. I wasn't sure how that was going to work.

And, honestly, there was part of me that *did* want him to find someone more suitable. I would be devastated if he did. Crushed. Heartbroken. And then very prolific in my writing. Crazy. But I also wanted what was best for him.

I texted him a picture of a leather sofa as a joke. He didn't reply. I wondered what he was doing. I wondered if he was with some young, handsome hunk and I'd never see him again. I wondered if I should see my shrink twice a week instead of just once because I was clearly nuts.

DORY

Confidential: I was seeing David twice a week. It was challenging because I really wanted to say, "Don't be a dumb fuck." But I didn't and won't. I kept my face expressionless, despite what my ex, Ronan (you didn't dare call him "Ron" or God forbid, "Ronnie") used to say about "the attitude in your eyes." Ronan was a shit and I hoped he was very happy with his young dental assistant Tiffy. I honestly did. Tiffy wasn't bright and probably deserved better but at least she was still young so she could divorce him and remarry before she was 30.

David spent over half of one session talking about upholstery. There were times when it was hard not to tune out and think about grilled salmon—but I didn't. That's why I took notes—to stay awake.

Here's one note I underlined three times, "It's fine if he fucks someone his own age but not my age, because then I'll be jealous." I told my own therapist, Selma, about this and she just shook her head. Neither of us knew what to say.

Then David talked about oral sex, which I wasn't in the mood to hear as it just reminded me of Ronan hissing, "Teeth, Dor-

dor, teeth!" At first I thought "Dor-dor" was cute. Then I hated it. I wonder if he calls her "Tif-tif." Poor girl.

LAWRENCE

I drove Cheyenne to the converted bus he called home. That's how he liked to live. He'd grown up in this bus that his father, Casper, had converted. His family didn't settle down in a log cabin until he was 16 and his mother, Dearie, said if she had to spend one more winter in the bus she'd burn Casper for warmth.

Cheyenne was studying agricultural management and his plan was to go back to Wyoming and tend to 50,000 acres of his family's "little ranch." Cheyenne loved cows and dreamily told me about being alone on a horse in the middle of nowhere. He said I needed to see the lay of the land and invited me to spend the night with him in his bus.

I thought about David. I had to draw the line somewhere because fucking counted as sex and I didn't want to cheat. I'd talk to David about it because he probably wouldn't mind unless it was a guy his age and then he'd be jealous. I know this because he said it in his sleep. He was whimpering and I tried to wake him and but he wouldn't wake up, he just kept repeating, "Don't fuck him, he's my age!" which I thought was weird but also funny. I love how funny he is!

David is crazy. He told me so. I hope that's not a problem.

DAVID

"We need to talk about sex," Lu texted me. I liked texting, because it was writing and therefore I could edit before I sent it, so I replied, "Oh no! Am I terrible?" I backspaced over it and instead sent, "Sure. What kind of sex?"

"Sex with other people," he replied and I swallowed hard. I figured this was coming but I didn't like the idea of it. At the same time, Dory had asked me if I'd be open to an open relationship (not with her, I think you have to be monogamous with your therapist, and I don't mean in the way Tedd was monogamous with Jez), and I said, "I don't know," because I didn't know.

In theory it sounded like a good idea. Sex *is* different than love, though it was beautiful when the two commingled. "Do you want an open relationship?" I typed, carefully, while Tedd in bed with Jez bounced around my brain.

"Given the situation I believe that would be the best course of action," he wrote that in that formal way he sometimes had that I chalked up to spending too many of his formative years in England where people talked like that, at least in period piece movies. I was very sensitive to the language used in dialog so to me it felt stilted but also very Lu.

What followed was two solid hours of texting until my thumbs were cramping and I had to resort to using the voice typing feature that always got things wrong. "But I rode you I above you."

Lu texted, "WTF?"

I loved that he used an *interrorbang* (?) after I explained what they were, but he was right, even I didn't know what that meant. Oh, "I told you I love you," I hurried to retype.

It got even worse because he'd text something and I'd start replying, then he'd send two more texts and now I was replying to something he'd said previously but he took it as a reply to what he'd just typed. It was unpleasant and confusing and it never occurred to me that we could actually use our phones to speak.

LAWRENCE

David didn't like talking on the phone. I knew he preferred to type so he could "compose his thoughts." That made sense as a writer but as a boyfriend it was bullshit. At one point I was crying because I said, "I'm fine with you seeing other people, too," just as his text came in and it said, "Dogs?" (I was trying to explain Cheyenne's tongue trick) and that got me thinking about cross-species stuff again which made me even more upset.

I was hurt and confused and should have called him but I didn't want to cry on the phone and sound like an emotional mess, which I was. I didn't like to involve other people in my messy emotions.

DORY

Confidential: David asked if he could do his sessions via text. I wanted to text him back with a 💩. Instead, I texted "🚫" It was important to have strong boundaries, though if we did our sessions via text I could have watched Downton Abbey at the same time. Not that I'd do that, but I could.

David said, "I don't like to involve other people in my messy emotions," and I replied, "It's called connection, David, as a writer I know you can understand that." He doesn't understand it. No wonder he's writing movies for children. I tried to watch one, Little Orphan Andrew, and the best thing I can say about it is that I slept for 20 minutes during the middle and I'm an insomniac. I now play the movie when I need to sleep.

DAVID

I was exhausted and I tried to end the conversation with this (I've copied and pasted verbatim).

> David 2:24am - If that's what you need then I support you.

I thought that would be the button on the scene. But no, he kept texting:

> Lawrence 2:24am - It sounds like you don't want it and are only doing it for my sake.

> David 2:25am - I want you to be happy.

> Lawrence 2:25am - That sounds like "goodbye."

> David 2:26am - OMG, it's not goodbye.

> Lawrence 2:26am - I want us to be happy!

> David 2:27am - I do, too, but maybe you'd be happier without me.

> Lawrence 2:27am - 😿😿😭

> David 2:28am - 😵😩... 😒WTF?

> Lawrence 2:29am - 🐝🥣💀🐝🥩🍪🧹

> David 2:29am - ????? I don't know what that means?

> Lawrence 2:29am - I was wiping tears off and accidentally hit the emojis.

> David 2:30am - but what do they mean?

> Lawrence 2:30am - that I'm crying because you want to break up!

I called him.

I apologized for not calling earlier.

I had to listen to him sobbing which broke my heart.

I told him I loved him, which was true.

He had to go to the bathroom to get toilet paper because he'd run out of Kleenex.

I told him I didn't care if it was Wednesday, I wanted to see him.

15 minutes later there he was, his eyes still red. I kissed him and held him and kept apologizing until he told me, "I forgive you, please stop now."

I sucked his cock. It tasted like tobacco. He told me about Cheyenne. I didn't let him see me cry.

LAWRENCE

"It's not even sex," I told him.

"Um, OK, sure..." he babbled.

"But you're jealous anyway."

"Not jealous. Scared." It always surprised me that such an accomplished man who was so sure of himself in his art could be so insecure in real life.

"Do you really think I'm such a flake that I'd leave you for a great blowjob from a cowboy?"

"You didn't say it was *great!*" he said, fighting back tears.

"This is the good part, we can learn new things and share them." I proceeded to show him Cheyenne's flat tongue technique, which he had a mostly positive reaction to. I never knew a man could cry and climax at the same time.

"This way we don't have to lie to each other, like Tedd lied to you," I explained, the mature one now.

"I know, I know, you're right. But that's what Tedd told me... I'm sorry to drag him into this, or to drag you into his shit, you don't deserve that."

"It's good," I told him, "I want you to feel free to share with me."

"And I want you to feel free to share your emotions with me. You can cry with me, right here. Not just when I'm being an asshole over text."

"No, I can't," I said, turning away, feeling weepy. "I want to, but... real men don't cry."

"Oh fuck yes they do."

"I never saw Cary Grant cry." I explained.

"What? He was a construct, a character. I'm sure he cried in real life with his boyfriend Randolph Scott."

"I want to be strong."

David wrapped his arms around me, he was, without a doubt, the best cuddler in the world. I liked the smell of his breath, too, chocolatey.

He whispered, "I support you in being whoever you want to be."

I fell asleep in his arms. The next day I talked to Dory about not wanting to cry in front of him and she said, "It's healthy to be able to show your vulnerabilities to your partner." Intellectually I believed her, but emotionally I still couldn't do it.

DORY

Confidential: Lawrence showed me a picture of Cheyenne on his phone. Woo wee, what a stud.

Then he told me he didn't want to cry in front of David— so they share that bit of emotional withholding at least. I said, "It's healthy to be vulnerable with your partner," which he took to be about David but I wonder if he's not better suited for Cheyenne. I can't say that, I just have to sit back and watch my patients make mistakes. Sigh.

DAVID

I've never been and never will be a cute cowboy. It's not in my wheelhouse. I did get aroused when Lu told me about what they did in the front seat of his car (which, incidentally, he and I have never done anything in, but then again my back can be iffy and it's way more comfortable on my leather sofa or in my bed).

I used to agree about kissing and sucking not counting as sex. But I keep having these flashbacks to Tedd and Jez— I know, I must stop. I talked with Dory about it and she said, "It's a natural part of the grieving process. The important thing is not to confuse Tedd's action with Lu's, they're two different people."

I subtly try to get her to talk about what Lu has told her. *I know* it's unethical and she can't and won't. I know that. But as a writer... oh, shit, as a boyfriend I want to know. It would be like a superpower— ah, yes, that's what I'm going to have the *Stunning Aliens* do—they can read minds (of course!) so they know what their lovers are really thinking. Or maybe that's too much and they just have super hearing so they can listen to their boyfriends talking on zoom. I'll have to think about it.

I am so unhappy now I'm writing like a madman, which is great and terrible. The alien piece is starting to come together. I wrote one entire scene where all anyone says is "fuck" in a great variety of ways (since the word can have so many meanings which are detailed in the stage directions). I should win some kind of award (an Oscar would be nice) for being able to forward the plot using only one word repeated over and over...

Cheyenne. Who's named that? Young Brad Pitt. I can't compete with that so I should simply stop trying. Lu can and should do whatever and whoever he wants. If he still wants me, then I'm lucky and I'll take it, but the more I think about it, the less I see how we could actually have a future together other than as a weekend FWB, friend with benefits.

I cry. I'm distraught. I write.

DORY

Confidential: David said, "I cry. I'm distraught. I write."

I asked, "How does that make you feel," which is what I say when, if I wasn't a professional, I'd smack him across the face. I didn't hear his answer. I feel bad about that.

LAWRENCE

Cheyenne invited me to dinner at a restaurant that uses steak from his family's ranch. I explained that I was a vegetarian. He said, "The cows only eat plants." He's very sweet but perhaps not the brightest thing.

Still... I checked the restaurant menu online and they had baked potatoes which I love, so I went with him and had mine with butter and sour cream and cheese and chives and it was delicious, with that kind of crispy skin you only get from baking for hours, which I generally don't have time for, so I microwave mine and it's not the same.

Cheyenne had a big steak, and I thought I'd be fine with it but it was very rare and bloody and I had to avoid eye contact with the meat because I felt sorry for it. I also understood how Cheyenne was raised but I didn't really want to make out with him in the car after, so we just sucked each other off.

DAVID

Marc noticed that I didn't make the shoe-shine boy white. I figured he would, but also figured he'd thank me for not doing what he asked. He did not thank me. He said, "I told you to change him," like I had a magic wand, though yes, that's what a pen can be for a writer.

I should note that I don't use a pen to write. My penmanship is unreadable. So I'm being metaphorical with the pen business when I really mean a keyboard, but that doesn't sound as romantic.

I was feeling more and more confident about the alien script so I told Marc, "I'm not changing it and you *will* thank me for it. If you don't like it, you can shove it up your racist ass." Then he made me put $1 in the swear jar on his desk, which was already stuffed.

"Where does all that money go?" I asked, innocently.

"My coke dealer."

"Happy to help, you motherfucker." I stuffed another dollar in the jar.

"Thanks. What's our next masterpiece" he asked me, popping a piece of nicotine gum in his mouth.

"I'm glad to see that you're trying to stop smoking."

"What're you talking about," he said, while chewing, "I just need more nicotine."

"I'm working on…" I stopped myself. I almost told him about the alien piece and he was the last producer on earth I wanted dealing with my space opera. I now envisioned it as "Star Wars with Smut!" Not a parody, but come on, it was all implied, I mean, "Princess *Leia*?" I rest my case.

Instead, I told him about a story I'd read in the paper. "There's this boy, Sean, only 12, but he was already working in an auto body shop because his mother was agoraphobic and wouldn't leave their trailer. Turns out Sean is a master with Bondo. He sees Diddy's Rolls Royce in the Whole Foods parking lot and it's got this little dent. On his own initiative he pops the dent, Diddy takes him under his wing and now he's the COO of Diddy Co."

Marc just stared at me. I couldn't tell if he's high or bored.

"In case you can't tell, I'm bored." he said, "Diddy is so 2006. No, no, no, no, no. Unless he's willing to do cross promo. But still no."

"You really are racist, aren't you, Marc?"

"I'm not a fucking racist you fucking idiot. I'm a capitalist."

"Ah, that explains it, thanks."

He shook his head sadly. "You're losing your touch, Dave. You used to come in here, full of vim and vigor without even needing coke. Now you drag your sorry old ass in…" (for the record, Marc was 46 and actually did have a sorry old ass which I'd only ever seen through the tight jeans he thought made him look younger) "…and tell me this cockamamie story. Where's the drama? The pathos? The orphan girl raised by her grandfather in the Alps!"

"You're thinking about Shirley Temple in Heidi," I told him. "80 years ago."

"Her shit still sells!" He stared me down as if that would convince me.

"Maybe I just need a little vacation, Marc. I've been pumping out scripts for 10 years now. Heartwarming has turned into heartburn."

"Yeah, I get it. Besides, there's a kid in the mail room, little Stevie Segal, who gave me his script about an orphan girl in the alps raised by her grandfather, only this is present day and she's built a robot dog named Alfie who's going to save them both in an avalanche. Sounds golden!"

"GoldMarc material for sure," I said, smiling because now maybe I was off the hook. It wasn't like anybody was forcing me to write clean comedies. I fell into the niche and did well doing it, but it was time for a change, for a new generation that would steal the plot of an 80 year old Heidi and update it with robotics. "I'll come back in a few months when I'm all refreshed," I said, not knowing if I was being honest or not, but it wasn't like Marc knew the difference. I was hedging my bets on the off chance that *Stunning Aliens* either didn't sell, or I had to go a Euro-Indie route with a low up-front and higher points which meant uncertain returns. Still, I was going to be an Oscar contender.

I saw a skinny kid carrying a skateboard enter Marc's office. His protege. Good luck!

DORY

Confidential: David told me he quit. At first I thought this was a good sign because now he could concentrate on his relationship with Lawrence. Instead, he's concentrating on his relationship with aliens. It doesn't sound healthy and on a personal note I wonder if he'll be able to continue to afford our sessions.

LAWRENCE

"You what?" I texted him when David texted me that he'd basically quit. That did not seem responsible to me.

"Now I can spend more time on *Stunning Aliens!*" he replied.

"Are you telling me that you're going to write more and see me less?" I typed, furiously.

There was a long pause with the animated "dot dot dots" moving, so I knew he was typing and editing and rewriting.

I finally saw, "The weekends are always yours, baby!"

I did not like him calling me *baby*. It felt infantilizing. I kept looking at his message, like he was doing me a favor by deigning to see me on weekends.

Fuck him! I felt my face get hot and I threw the phone on my bed. The same bed where I planned to spite fuck somebody else tonight.

I called Yasmin. It rang a long time. When she finally picked up I blurted, "Can you fucking believe it?"

"No, I can't, Bruno's been down there for 20 minutes and now it's just irritating."

"I called about David!"

"You always call about David."

"Nothing's changed."

"What did you expect, Boo?" she said as I heard grunts in the background. "Bruno, stop, I'm on the phone!"

"It's been three months of the same weekend shit. I thought he'd get over it!" I explained, distracted by the bull sounds Bruno was making. "What are you doing right now?" I asked her, getting mad at her, too.

"I was watching *Project Runway* when you called, then Bruno came in and got on his knees acting like I was his personal buffet. Bruno, stop, please, you're blocking my view of the TV!"

"I'll call you later when you're not getting eaten out," I told her, annoyed.

"Bruno, go make yourself a sandwich," she yelled. "Sorry, Boo Boo, it wasn't my idea. Fine, he's gone and I've turned off the TV. Spill."

"Why am I waiting around for him?" I asked her, almost crying because I was both sad and angry.

"Don't ask me. He's old and not my type at all. But he did write *Plain Jane*," she reminded me.

"Yeah, but now he's writing something dirty about aliens."

She whispered, "Bruno likes me to pretend to be an alien giving him anal probes," she giggled.

"I don't need to hear stuff like that," I protested.

"Why not, you tell me all about your little friend Cheyenne and his doggie tongue, though, I have to say, that's a good technique and it's a standard part of my repertoire now."

"I need to cuddle," I whined. I didn't like how it sounded when I whined but I did it anyway because it worked.

"Then get your cute little ass over here, pronto. I'll tell Bruno to beat it, which he'll take to mean 'beat it off' which he likes to do outside in the hydrangeas. Yeah, I know, I don't know what I saw in him. Come over now and we'll commiserate about bad boyfriends!"

I hung up and thought about what to wear. On one hand, I'd known Yasmin since the first day of university, so I could come over in sweats. On the other hand, Yasmin was very chic, and she'd only be comfortable if the sweats were cashmere.

I decided on spandex workout shorts and hoodie because I'd lost three pounds worrying and felt cute. Besides, Yasmin always complimented me on my legs.

I rang her doorbell and waited. The hydrangea by the door shook. I sneaked a look. Nope, Bruno the bull was not my type. Yasmin answered the door and I pointed to the hydrangeas. "He'll be occupied for an hour, then he'll fall asleep there so we have plenty of time."

Talk about cute— she wore a pink satin nightgown with fuzzy marabou trim and gold sandals with green gems in them. I could tell immediately the gems were fake, but it was all about the effect.

"You look fab," I told her, spinning her around to see her backside.

"Your legs are magic, Boo" she returned the compliment.

She looked genuinely hot. "If you had a dick I'd fuck you right now."

"You have a dick and we really only need one," she said, seductively.

The next thing I knew we were making out— she's the one who taught me the right way to kiss when I was 18 and I taught her the right way to give a blow job. I'm sure our boyfriends were eternally grateful.

"You're such a fucking great kisser," she told me when my mouth wasn't on hers.

"I learned from the master!" I replied.

"Now I'll show you what *I* learned from *you*," she said, peeling off my spandex pants.

I wanted to say, "You have learned well, young Jedi," but she was, in fact, so good that I couldn't speak.

Then things got weird, and on her white bouclé wool sofa, too.

"Fuck me with your beautiful dick, Lutfullah!" I loved the way she said my name. I loved her. Not in a romantic way but in a "We've been best friends for a decade and you look ridiculously hot tonight," kind of way.

For once I didn't think about the sofa fabric. She spread her legs and I slid into her— the first time I'd ever fucked a woman... I briefly thought about David, "we never said I couldn't fuck a woman," before the thought floated away with our groans. She was soft and wet and I now *almost* understood the appeal of being a straight man.

The combination of this taboo union, and how pretty she was, and how angry I was, and how reckless I felt with this upholstery sent me over the edge and I found myself shooting into her over and over... then immediately feeling guilty.. "I'm sorry, I'm so sorry, I didn't think I'd..."

"That's OK, Boo. Our baby will be gorg," she smiled.

I cried. What had I done? Was this going to ruin our friendship? Besides, I wanted to be the one to have the baby!

"Oh, Boo. I was just kidding, I'm on the pill. It's fine. Better than fine because you're a surprisingly good fuck."

That made me laugh. "It was my first time with a girl."

"I'd never have known—I'm honored. And I thought you were a bottom." She kissed me again. She was a great kisser. "We are the perfect couple," Yasmin said, her cheeks flushed.

"Almost perfect," I kissed her back. "Is this going to fuck up our friendship?"

"Fuck no! Now we can be friends with benefits!" she said, excitedly. "I've gotten very good at anal probes," she whispered.

"In that case, maybe..." I whispered back before falling to sleep.

DAVID

Lu didn't respond to my texts. I called and it went to voicemail.

It was Friday night, I'd made enchiladas Alfredo and I'd heard nothing from him.

So that was it. I ate the entire tray of enchiladas, felt nauseous and sad and depressed and wrote 20 pages of my screenplay in one sitting.

I imagined Lu having sex with anything that moved, and it inspired a scene where Zorn did, too. The goldfish scene was total silliness. Mating with a killer whale was majestic.

I was a genius. An old, fat, always-to-be-alone genius.

I didn't hear from him all weekend. I was halfway through my script.

LAWRENCE

I woke up alone on her sofa. I checked for stains, mentally ready to go out and buy upholstery cleaning foam if necessary. It wasn't necessary.

David had sent so many text messages I just skipped down to the last one which said, "It's OK I understand."

I don't think he did.

"I've convinced Bruno to go back to Spain..." Yasmin told me. "...to take care of his aged mother and run the family cheese business. He'll be gone for at least six months. What a relief. Now you and I can be a thing."

I heard her but it didn't register.

"Uh huh," I said. We'd always been a thing, just not a TWB, a thing with benefits. "I gotta go," I mumbled.

"Of course, it's Friday night, go have fun with David," she said, giving me a full on mouth kiss. She tasted like strawberry.

I left in a daze.

YASMIN

Oh my God. OH my God! OH MY GOD! Who knew my little gay would be a great lay.

I've always joked that we made the perfect couple but I never thought anything would happen. But when it did— he was so fucking good. And beautiful. And sweet.

I've never been one of those girls who started to think about the wedding, no, that'd be silly. But I could imagine us all dressed up, out on the town—we'd look great together! I could see us fucking in the back of a town car. My parents would love him.

I had to stop myself from fantasizing about the two of us on a nude beach in Mykonos, glancing lovingly at each other with the scent of the sea in our noses and the sparkle of love in our eyes.

He'd make me beautiful jewelry and I'd make him beautiful babies.

Maybe this was just a one-time thing.

No, we'd been friends for ages and he was hurt and vulnerable and I could work with that! He already loved me, I knew it, but now he could really love me.

No, no, no, couldn't go there yet. He was gay, he'd always be gay. He'd always be my best friend. I'd find a straight man who wasn't a pig and he and I and Boo and David or Cheyenne would all travel together.

It was fun. It would never happen again.

Unless I made it.

DAVID

I waited till Monday to text Lu, "Is that it?"

Now the misery was getting in my way. I checked the phone obsessively instead of writing. Then I saw the animated "dot dot dot" of his typing. His beautiful fingers putting together words, just for me.

"I'm very confused." That was it. No more dot dot dot.

I saw an entire scenario in my head. He was in Wyoming, fucking Cheyenne on horseback. They had an army surplus Jeep and a sheep dog named *Shep* and a Shetland pony named *Pinkie*.

Cheyenne went hunting and brought home wild carrots. Lu scoured the land for gold nuggets and shiny stones with which he created the world's finest cowboy belt buckles. They were deliriously happy together.

I told myself I was happy for him but it was a lie. I was furious with myself and made a big batch of tahini chocolate chip cookies and ate the dough raw, a self-destructive act if there was salmonella in the eggs, and fattening if not.

I couldn't even think about the aliens.

I was furious with myself. How could I have been so stupid? I was going to die lonely, maybe tonight as the dough gave me painful gas that wouldn't come out, so I rocked back and forth, moaning.

LAWRENCE

Yasmin texted. "I love you, Boo." That's a relief. I don't know what I was thinking. Well, I wasn't thinking, I had no blood in my brain. We're very flawed as animals that way.

I loved her, too. I wondered if it wouldn't be easier to marry her and have a normal family. Would my family be relieved? Would I be relieved? It seemed easier. We could hold hands anywhere and people would say, "Isn't that sweet," instead of "Isn't that disgusting."

But I could remember my uncle Fareed saying, "I'm happy to be gay, and you will be, too."

YASMIN

"You can still fuck men once we're married :)" I texted him. I wasn't joking. He could. I could. That was basically perfect. There

were always handsome artists coming into the gallery. Handsome rich patrons of the arts, too.

Boo could stay home raising the children and designing jewelry and I could mix with artists and the rich men who feel special when they buy their art from a beautiful young curator.

OMG, what am I thinking? I must stop. But my mother called and asked who I was seeing and I said, "Lutfullah" and mother said, "It's about fucking time, girl!" Then I heard dad hooting in the background.

I'm not this kind of woman. I am strong. I am invincible. I am in love.

CHEYENNE

Holy fucking shit, man!

Larry showed up outta the blue, knocked me on the floor and fucked me like a fucking animal.

Fucking stud made me see big sky stars. I ain't never felt that before.

"Dude, you're a fucking animal!" I told him, limping like I just broke a stallion, but that shit was totally bomb diggity.

LAWRENCE

"Oh, fuck. Not this again. What kind of animal do you want me to be?" I said wearily to Cheyenne.

"No, I'm not into freaky things, Larry..." I liked the way he said, "Larry," even though I normally hated that name. "I just mean that you're fucking awesome."

We cuddled up together. I liked his muscular arms. I didn't hate the bus, either.

DAVID

Yasmin sent *me* a text message, "Lu fucked me. We're in love. Back off, Bitch."

I didn't see that one coming.

It was Friday night again, and I hadn't heard from him and now I knew why.

"I wish you both every happiness," I texted back to her, sobbing on the sofa—loud, ugly crying. I knew it was inevitable. He was too good for me, the way I used to think Tedd was too good for me.

I tortured myself looking at pictures of Lu on my phone. Shit. His eyes. His lips. His heart!

I loved everything about him. Everything. There wasn't one thing about him I could find fault with. Except for him fucking a woman and I didn't even think that was his fault—I bet Yasmin seduced him. I mean, who wouldn't seduce him?

But Lu was more than just another pretty face and pretty ass. He had depth. He was smart and funny and sweet and made me feel... seen. That was it.

Tedd was always the one people saw, at least in terms of how he looked. I was the nerdy writer. Even when someone said something nice, like, "We loved *Apple Pie Betty*," they'd say it while staring at Tedd's perfect stalactite teeth.

When they were out of earshot, I was sure they talked about Tedd's teeth and not about how hard I worked on that script about Betty, the poor orphan girl who's sharecropper father died in a tragic farm equipment accident yet still went on to find fame by baking her own world-renowned pies with their 11-teen secret herbs and spices that were sold across six Southern states and the Eastern Seaboard.

LAWRENCE

I'd memorized the 11-teen secret herbs (rosemary) and spices (white pepper, coconut, ginger, hibiscus, nutmeg, orange peel, cinnamon, nutmeg, star anise, and cloves). David and I made a pie using his recipe from the movie and it was delicious.

He was truly special. Too bad he was crazy and was more interested in his writing than me. Yasmin is definitely more interested in me. I wanted that.

DAVID

I thought about the pie we made together. I remembered how he looked at me with love. I realized what I'd lost. I cried. I baked. I ate. I felt stuffed and sad.

DORY

Confidential: David cried throughout our session. And burped. It was hard to watch, partly because I felt sorry for him, and partly because it was pathetic and his own fault.

I suggested that the way to heal was to own his own decisions.
He could study his actions as if he was a character in one of his
screenplays. "Ask yourself why that character made that
stupid-ass decision?" I didn't use the words "stupid-ass" I just
thought them. At least I think I just thought them. Did I say
them? It concerns me that I'm not sure.

DAVID

Dory said I needed to look at myself like a character in one of my screenplays. OK. "David loved nothing more than writing— entering his own private world where anything was possible and everything made sense. His real life was kind of a mess but at least it looked good." Oh my God! This is the most boring thing I've ever written. I am the most boring human alive!

"Be kind to yourself," Dory said practically every week while only looking slightly annoyed. I once said, "You look slightly annoyed," and she said "Is that how *you* think I look? Let's talk about that." I ended up talking about my mother and crying.

So I'll try to be kind to my boring self. No, not boring. Introverted? Uh... Unrealistic? Uh... Fucking idiot? Yes, that sounds right.

How could I care more about writing fiction than real-live-Lu? Maybe because my fictional world was always safe. My characters didn't leave me the way I knew Lu would.

DORY

Confidential: "Self-fulfilling prophecy," is what I told David.
"When you write, you create what you focus on. With Lu, you
focused on failure, and that's what you created.."

I don't think I was being too harsh.

"You can learn from this experience with someone new," I
suggested—gently—because, while I couldn't tell David what Lu
said, it was clear to me that Lu was hurt, angry and done.

By "someone new" I also meant a new therapist. ""Look at it as
a tabula rasa," I said cheerfully, explaining that I was going to
a month-long silent retreat in Nova Scotia. It was something
I'd been considering ever since David started as a client.

SHELLI

I questioned just how professional it was for David's shrink to
leave, given his abandonment issues. But I was glad I'd have
more time with him.

As he lay with his head in my lap, I fed him "La Madeleine au
Truffe" chocolates I had flown in from The House of Knipschildt.

Once he was suitably anesthetized, I cut right to the chase, "You
fucked up, my love. Learn from it and move forward." He started
to cry again but I wasn't sure if it was about Lu or the fact that
the chocolate box was empty.

I had Hiroto bring another box of chocolates. David continued to cry, so it was about Lu.

"You need to get laid, bubeleh," I told him, as he left with the box of truffles. I texted him a link to the app Hiroto swore by.

DAVID

I would learn from this experience—yes! Hard-won knowledge, for sure.

I downloaded the Scruff gay dating app Shelli had texted me with the words, "Hint, hint!" She had the magical ability to tell me just the right thing at just the right time, which might also have been because I told her things I didn't even tell Dory. Mostly sex things because Shell found them fascinating while I felt like Dory looked uncomfortable, but that could just be me projecting.

I created an account in the app and uploaded the best photos of myself, taken by Scavullo, 15 years ago. He'd made me look like a movie star, or at least a b-movie star. Beautiful black and white portraits with dramatic lighting.

Even I would have been attracted to that guy! Then I looked in the mirror. If I wanted the guy in the picture but met the current me I'd be confused/disappointed/angry. Delete. Delete. Delete.

I uploaded a semi-recent publicity headshot taken by Joyce St. Rudolph, the still photographer on the set of *Abacus Dreams*. That wasn't one of my best titles as nobody outside of Asia knew what an abacus was anymore. Nor did they seem to care about a 12-year-old mathematics prodigy who harbored the secret ambition to be a tap dancer.

This wasn't a bad headshot. It made me look as good as I was going to look without the kind of retouching where my head was actually replaced with someone else's.

I wrote a short profile: "Successful screenwriter and teddy bear seeks fellow creative cuddler. Looking for a real connection but am not adverse to extremely hot sex. The reviews are in, "*****" — The New York Times." "Delightful from beginning to end! — Rotten Tomatoes." "I watched it 27 times — Lu." "I came twice—Tedd from West Hollywood."

With that done I searched for nearby men who didn't look like 1) trolls, 2) troglodytes, 3) me.

I saw a cute cub... a little chubby but I couldn't complain about that. Very cute. A bit fem, wearing a tiara thing. His profile said... oh, wait, *their* profile said, "Creative non-binary who digs creative daddy types." Hmm, sounded promising. "Inquire within." That made me laugh.

I messaged him, "Hey, Cub! Inquiring minds want to know" and pressed "send."

I put the phone down and started dinner, hamburgers with smoked paprika.

The phone chimed. "Hey daddy-o! Cute face. Cool profile. Whatcha like?"

The first burger burned while we messaged back and forth.

"You hungry?" I typed.

"Is that a euphemism?" he replied. Ooh, he had a multisyllabic vocabulary—a good sign!

"No and yes. I'm making burgers and then hopefully making you."

"I haven't eaten for hours. What's your address?"

I thought about it for a few seconds. A stranger coming to my house? Maybe he wasn't even the guy in the picture. Maybe he was a 50 year old ex-con from Visalia who was going to kill me and steal my Fiat. Killing me would be bad enough.

Yes, he'd sent me his Instagram link, and there were a lot of pictures of him in various colorful outfits. He looked super cute in a pink and blue plaid miniskirt with knee-high rainbow socks.

Let's see, possible murderer or possible cute boy. I typed my address, "... The white Spanish house just south of the intersection of Waring and Orange." Send.

"See ya soon!"

I turned down the grill low, just in case he was hungry for something else first. He was.

CUBBY

I recognized David from pictures on Lawrence's phone. I knew they had an open relationship so it was no biggie.

Nice house. Dramatic outdoor lighting, the succulents cast spiky shadows on the rough plaster walls. Cool pattern—I took a pic so I could use it on a poncho.

David was cute in a lux normcore dad kind of way— wearing cargo sweats but in good quality merino wool.

He asked me if I wanted to eat. I said later. He seemed shy. I kissed him with a lot of tongue. He tasted like paprika, which I love.

We played on his black leather sofa which made squeaking noises when we got sweaty. He was a sensual man, touching me lightly and giving me goosebumps. He was a good top, too, not too big, "fun size" he joked, but seriously comfortable, and passionate. And he had staying power. I didn't time it or anything but I could hear *Real Housewives of Grand Rapids* coming from the TV in the other room so it must have been at least an hour and a half.

"I like you," I said, playing with his beard. "You're one hot daddy."

His face twitched into a smile.

DAVID

"One hot daddy," he said. I still hadn't gotten used to being called "daddy" but he… (I knew better than to misgender *them* but sometimes I still forgot) …*they* clearly meant it in a good way, so I just said, "Thanks, you're a hot cub, too."

We cuddled and I was surprised at how nice it was. I mean, I was used to Lu who was more fit, but Cubby's soft edges were perfect for cuddling. Maybe that's something Lu had liked about me. I thought about him for a few minutes as Cubby snored like a puppy. I felt bad about losing Lu, but I hoped he'd found someone less crazy.

I peeled myself off Cubby, washed my hands and got the burgers ready for the grill. He… sorry, *they*, shuffled in, wearing only their pink flowered boxers. They kissed my spatula hand and I put the burgers on.

As we ate they told me about their budding fashion business. "I sell everything through Etsy. I usually sell out the same day they drop." I was impressed at their creativity and enterprise. "So you really wrote *Plain Jane?*"

"Yup. And 22 two other comedies that have grossed over 100 million at the box office and on video." I didn't mean to spout stats but I was trying to remember myself what I'd accomplished, to boost my own confidence.

"What're you writing now?" they asked, a question I usually hated. It didn't matter what I'd done, all that mattered was what I'd do next. Still, they meant it innocently, so I explained about *Stunning Aliens.*

"Oh, my God! I fucking love that! Tell me what your aliens look like?"

I mentioned Jez and Salma, and Cubby started sketching with a knife dipped in ketchup. "I can totally see them like this!" Their sketch was remarkably well done for being made of tomato, and I understood the style immediately — androgynous, like David Bowie meets Cher but in space.

"What's that coming out of *their* head?" I asked, careful about pronouns. At first I had a really hard time with "they" and "them" being singular. It just felt wrong. Then somebody explained to me, "You already say things like 'what are they doing?' when you're talking about an individual, so it's the same thing."

I knew that language was powerful and this was the power that non-binary people wanted and needed. Sometimes I still slipped, I almost said, "you're a cute boy," but I managed to leave it at "You're cute."

They left the table and came back wearing a long sparkly blue tunic with a kangaroo pocket in front. They pulled out a pen and a little notebook and started making more sketches.

"I can imagine them from a sea planet, so they're wearing a lot of blues and greens, and their eyes change colors to match their clothes. Flowy clothes that move like they're underwater. Their long blue hair flows and changes color, too. I like the idea that they can be whatever color they want, so they get along with all ethnicities."

I watched in wonder as Cubby gave shape to my characters. "Do they have genitals?" they asked.

I had naively assumed they were male and female. "They have both?" I said, not sure how that worked, but hey, they're aliens!

"That would be cool. Being underwater in their home world has more pressure so in our light atmosphere they need tight-fitting bondage stuff to hold themselves together."

"You're hired, kid!" I said. "Seriously, I want to pay you to do concept art for the pitch package."

"Coolio, daddio! When it gets produced I want to do the costumes."

LAWRENCE

My phone pinged and woke me up at 3am. The yellow light of the street lamps came through the bus windows. It took me a while to remember where I was. Cheyenne was splayed out in a loincloth. We'd played cowboys and Indians and I enjoyed playing the cowboy for a change while he was the Indian even if it was politically incorrect.

The text was from Cubby. "David's a super hot daddy. Your loss is my gain. Goodnight!"

Shit! Why was I jealous? Because they were perfect for each other? Cheyenne was cute and sexy, but was he more interested in cows than culture?

Good for Cubby. And David.

I felt like crap. I started drawing a necklace inspired by barbed wire with brown tiger eye cabochons like cow patties. It was beautiful. Being unhappy made me want to be creative. Shit, now I understood what David meant!

YASMIN

Boo and I went to the theater and saw a musical about two drag queens who had a happy family. I was glad Boo wasn't into that kind of flamboyant feminine stuff. He looked straight. And so pretty.

During one of the big dance numbers I ran my hand down his thigh and felt him get hard.

Look, I get it, you're born gay. Nobody can really turn you gay or straight. But maybe Boo didn't know he was bi because he'd never had sex with a girl. Now that he'd experienced sex with me, he could be bi!

The thing is, I'd always loved him. Actually loved him. Yes, as a friend, but also as a man. I'd never met another man who was as kind, generous, thoughtful, or sweet.

We went to a bar after the show and both had a few Appletinis and were feeling fine. I ordered an Uber Black SUV and straddled him in the back seat, each bump from a pothole making me gasp.

LAWRENCE

I love Yasmin— always have. Last night after we fucked in the back of an Uber (which was hot and mortifying at the same time), she asked, "Have you ever thought that you might be bi?"

I never had. But clearly I must have been, since I got excited by her.

I still thought about David—but he'd pushed me away, hadn't he? He told me to fuck other people—yes he did. He was with Cubby now.

So why did I keep scrolling through my photos with David and feeling sad? I asked Dory about it and she said, "You need to have this conversation with him."

I said, "OK," to appease her. But I didn't think I would.

DAVID

I was looking at photos of Lu on my phone when there was a knock at the door. Nobody ever knocked on the door here, except people selling things, so I was going to ignore it. My curiosity got the best of me and I peeked out a window. Oh my God.

Tedd was standing at my door looking especially Ralph Lauren with a tweed blazer and contrasting vest, rust and blue plaid shirt and pressed jeans with cowboy boots. The sun was setting behind his head, making him picture perfect.

I couldn't stop myself from opening the door a crack. "What do you want?" I asked warily.

"Please let me in, Davey, I need you."

That's exactly what I'd fantasized he'd say.

In those fantasies I always said, "Go away, you ugly loser," because this was the worst thing I could think of to say to him.

But as I stared at him, his perfection faded. He'd gained weight and his face was puffy and red. So all I said was, "I'm writing." I felt bad because he looked like he needed help, but as Dory and I had discussed, he was no longer my responsibility.

"I'm sorry. I'm sorry for everything, Davey," he said, sniffling and blowing his nose on one of the monogrammed handkerchiefs I'd given him— clearly coded language. "Please, please, please," he whispered. Those were words I'd so rarely heard from him in the past that it was as if he'd said, "Open Sesame."

I opened the door. He slumped in and put his arms around me, feeling heavier than I remembered.

"Let's sit you down," I said, leading him to the leather sofa where his presence would be mitigated by my memories of the sex that I'd recently had there.

"I'm an idiot," he said, once again flourishing the monogrammed hankie as if to say, "Yes, I remember how good you were to me."

"I always knew that," I said unkindly.

"You always did, and you loved me anyway."

I thought about his words. Had I ever loved him? It was hard to imagine now. OK, not that hard but I didn't want to imagine it.

"I've loved you since that first day I met you," he sniffled. "Jez brainwashed me."

"At least you have a clean brain now." I felt bad about being mean. This was a man I had loved. Or had thought I loved. Or still loved. I didn't really know.

"I miss you, Davey." He looked up at me with his tear-filled blue-green eyes and my mind was flooded with sweet memories.

TEDD

After 10 years I thought I could do better. That sounds mercenary and awful, I know. Davey was a nice guy, a creative guy, but always chubby. I liked that at first, he was great to cuddle. But I went to the gym and worked hard on my pecs, abs and glutes and most of my friends and customers did the same.

I tried to get Davey to go to the gym with me, but he didn't like to sweat, and he found it all boring. "But you're doing something important, you're building your body," I'd tell him and he'd joke, "I'll stick to Wonder bread, that helps build strong bodies 12 ways." He liked to say stuff he thought was funny then he'd explain to me about the history of Wonder bread and its 12 added vitamins. We were the same age but he'd watched a lot of TV as a kid while I was out on the tennis court.

OK, so I'd dress him in Ralph Lauren. He looked... cute... but he looked 41 and I looked... 29.

Fuck, I know now how shallow I was. But helping men look good was my business, so I had to look good myself, and when I'd launch a collection I'd have to make a few pieces in larger sizes just for Davey and he wasn't exactly aspirational.

He'd say, "You know, Teddy, if you made clothes in bigger sizes you'd double your business. There's not much competition in stylish larger sizes." I thought about it, but then figured the guys who looked like me wouldn't want to buy from a brand that made clothes for guys who looked like him.

I should have listened. Instead, I listened to Jez when he said I needed to expand my business... partly because he wasn't making enough to live in the style to which he wanted to be accustomed.

Jez convinced me to make a line of colorful cardigans like the ironically ugly ones his granny knitted. I spent a ton on mohair and samples—nobody bought them. Not Saks, Mr. Porter, Farfetch, Harvey Nichols, not even Nordstrom's, Bloomingdale's or, gasp, Macy's. When they didn't think I was looking, I saw buyers laugh.

I lost money and gained weight.

Then I came home and found Jez in bed with a very strange man. Jez said, "It's not what it looks like, Tedster."

What it looked like was Jez fucking Fred Flintstone. What else could it have been?

Tedd kept talking, "Oh, sorry. Ignacio, this is my partner Tedd. Tedd, this is my new patient, Ignacio."

I was pretty sure I'd seen Ignacio on a Netflix documentary about the ten most wanted drug lords. I could have been wrong, I wasn't seeing straight, but I did know he wasn't my type and I wasn't interested.

I felt like I was going to shit my pants because I saw exactly what I'd done to Davey who didn't deserve it, just as I didn't deserve it.

"I'm going to get your sorry ass disbarred, or whatever happens to therapists," I growled.

"I'm not licensed, so I'm not doing anything wrong. Besides, this counts as sex therapy."

I'd never felt more stupid in my entire life of feeling stupid and hiding it well under nice clothes.

I went to the second bedroom that we'd converted into a closet, changed clothes, left my dirty underwear on the floor, changed into one of my newer, bigger outfits that fit more comfortably, packed three large bags and left. I took his Lamborghini and parked it in the deepest underground parking garage in Century City where the GPS tracker wouldn't work. Then I took a Lyft back to his house and drove my Jaguar away, too. I was finally learning from Davey.

Now I found myself standing at Davey's door, crying like the idiot I was. I knew he'd take me in, and he did.

LAWRENCE

Much as I loved Yasmin, thinking about a future with her made me miss David. I wanted him back.

I was just getting out of my car when I saw a Jaguar drive up and out came Tedd, looking perfect as he did in all the pictures Davey never deleted from his phone.

Tedd knocked on the door. David let him in. I thought I heard him say, "I've missed you, too."

Oh, so that's how it was now. Maybe that's how it always was! Maybe David was always cheating on me with Tedd! Maybe they were both laughing at me!

My rational brain dissolved into a puddle of self-pity! I was a laughingstock again, like when all those kids at school mocked my accent before I learned to sound like them!

What made me think I was good enough for the handsome, successful and funny man who wrote *Plain Jane?*

Yasmin was right! She said she was the best thing that had ever happened to me. I was lucky she'd even have me and my giant eyebrows. I was lucky she could give me a normal family and kids.

I got back in my car and drove back to her.

DAVID

Tedd told me his tale of woe which at first left me cold— what's good for the goose is good for the gander and all that cliche... oh, no, now I was the cliche so I didn't deserve to be all high and mighty.

Besides, I could see he was in pain, the way I'd been in pain, and I could tell he understood the terrible, horrible, unforgivable mistake he'd made— and I forgave him.

I didn't mean to. I meant to be mean. I meant to throw him out on his perky ass and laugh, triumphantly. I meant to show him how strong I'd become, forged by fire! I could even envision the shot of me, the setting sun streaming from behind making me look mythic!

But seeing him sniffle on the sofa where I'd fucked cute guys I wouldn't have fucked if Tedd hadn't fucked Jez, I thought, "Maybe this was for the best. Maybe it's a kind of reset and we can go back to the nice life we had, except maybe open so I can still have..."

That's when I thought of Lu. I should have thought of Cubby who was cute and talented and liked me, but I thought of Lu. Poo.

LAWRENCE

Cheyenne was scooting around on all fours, barking like a dog. If he'd thought this was sexy I would have run, but he was merely demonstrating how his hound found gophers. It was both dumb and endearing.

He stood on his 'hind legs' holding a pair of socks in his mouth, shaking his head wildly. "Max shakes them until they're dead, you should see it!" he said, joyously.

"I don't really want to see that," I found myself saying.

"Yeah, I get that it's hard for a city boy like you but it's nature, Lare, that's how it works."

He had a point, and I was getting closer to being convinced to go with him to Wyoming because the pictures he showed me were stunning. Cheyenne was a fine photographer, not just "Instagram good" but "artistically good," with a level of talent and refinement that turned me on.

Plus, I'd be further away from David and less likely to think about him and Tedd back together again. It made me mad that David would be so stupid as to take that asshole back. Then it made me mad that I'd be so stupid as to want a man who'd take Tedd back. So why should I take David back?

Cheyenne... I really needed a nickname for him. "Hey, Shy..." I tried. He didn't respond. "You need a nickname, so I'm going to call you..."

"Benny, that's my nickname back home."

"What? How do you get Benny from Cheyenne?"

"My middle name's Ben, so Benny."

I liked Shy better. "Can I still call you *Shy*?" I asked, batting my long eyelashes.

"You can call me anything you want, Lare, just don't call me late for dinner!" he said, pulling a package of hot dogs out of the cooler and throwing them on a cast iron grill. This was his idea of dinner. "I bought you some *FakeFurters*, made out of beans or something," he said, smiling radiantly. It was times like this I wished he wasn't so fucking handsome.

"Thanks, Shy," I said, because it was thoughtful for him to buy something vegetarian for me even though they tasted like burnt peas. He didn't answer. "Thanks, Benny."

"You betcha, Lare!"

TEDD

I slept on the sofa that first night back. It smelled funny, like Davey had spilled something on it. I found some dried white residue under a cushion. Probably Alfredo sauce.

CUBBY

I wanted to surprise David, so I snuck through his bedroom window which I knew he liked to keep open. I slipped into bed and he nearly freaked out. "What the fuck... Get out!"

I'm not prone to tears, I've been through way too much to cry easily anymore, except at YouTube videos with cats or babies. But I started to cry.

"I wanted to surprise you," I wept, sitting on the edge of the bed.

"Oh, Cubby, it's you."

"Who were you expecting? Do you have a repertory company of lovers?" Even as I cried I wondered why I was so upset. I'd only seen him a few times. It was fun, but not serious. Still, I felt seriously rejected, and that was an old wound that still hadn't healed.

"No, I thought you were someone else."

"That makes it so much better. I'm sorry to have bothered you, I'm going now."

He jumped out of bed, surprisingly spry for a man of 50, and held me. "Come on back, Cubby. I'll explain."

I didn't like explanations, which were more often than not excuses. But he told me about how his ex was sleeping on the sofa and it actually sounded like an explanation, especially after he said, "I'm happy to see you, Cub."

He held me, which I needed, and told me the whole ugly story of Tedd. "So why are you taking him back? I would have kicked him out on his ass, no matter how cute an ass it was."

"That's what I thought I'd do, too, but we have too much history... and now that he's suffered I can forgive him."

"You're a better man than I, Gunga Din," I said.

He squeezed me tight. "I love that you know that line. You're a very special... *person*." he said. I could tell he almost called me a man, and I wouldn't have been upset by that because he made me feel masculine in a way I didn't feel in the world.

"Spend the night, please. I'll introduce you to Tedd in the morning. That should give him some perspective on what he can expect."

I really dug this dude.

DAVID

I thought Tedd had gotten in bed with me and I wasn't ready for that. Turned out to be Cubby, and I yelled at him and watched him melt into a wounded boy. It was a sad but beautiful moment that I was going to use in the Alien script.

I liked this kid. In some ways he reminded me of myself. I know it sounds weird but that also turned me on. I remember reading a book called "The Man Who Folded Himself," when I was 12. The protagonist was a time traveler who went back in time and had sex with himself. That got me off many times in my formative years.

Being with Cubby felt a little bit like that. More than a little bit. A lot.

At first I tried to be quiet, I didn't want to wake Tedd. Then I thought, "maybe it's best if he walks in on us." Then I thought that was mean. Then I was in the throes of passion and didn't care.

The gay couples I knew were either like Cubby and me, guys who could pass for brothers, or twins... or, no, wait, in this case, father and son? Anyway, they tend to either look alike, or look totally different, like me and Tedd.

I held Cubby while he slept and remembered the nights when Tedd held me this way.

TEDD

I woke up to a baby version of David in a baby doll nightie over a rainbow jockstrap clomping around in Doc Martens. I wondered if I'd fallen asleep on a stranger's sofa. I looked around. No, this was our house. I still thought of it as ours.

I was just about to say, "Hey, princess, who the fuck are you?" when Davey appeared, took the princess by the hand and led him or her or them to me.

"Ted, this is Cubby. He's my boyfriend."

CUBBY

"Boyfriend." That's what D called me. In front of his ex who looked like a male model circa the 1990 International Male catalog. Not to say he was old, but he reminded me of that "Mr. Worthington" male model on Instagram who's got a crooked smile and a lot of silver hair.

I blushed.

In this case, I didn't mind being called a "boy," but later I'd I'd have to tell him the non-binary alternatives, like *goyfriend*, which I don't particularly like because I'm not a goy. *Lover* was better.

TEDD

"Boyfriend," Davey said.

"Lover is the non-binary term," the so-called boyfriend said.

I didn't know what to say, so I just made a face, something I don't do often because it leads to wrinkles.

David noticed. "You left me..."

I didn't want to argue about who left, since he was the one who left, but I admitted I was to blame. "...you're right, I have no right. Hello, young lover, whoever you are."

DAVID

My jaw dropped. Tedd was quoting a song title from *The King and I?* That's something I used to do and now he was doing it. I was so proud.

TEDD

I didn't realize till I said it that I was quoting the title from one of the musicals Davey had listened to obsessively when we were younger.

"So are we a thruple?" I asked.

"What? No. He's mine," Davey announced defensively, pulling the *person* close to him.

I said, "Oh," because I couldn't think of anything else to say. I also couldn't fault him for it.

"You're not my type," the mini-Davey said in a high light voice that was both sweet and hurtful.

Then nobody said anything.

DAVID

I looked at Cubby and smiled. I liked that Tedd wasn't his type. This was going to be interesting.

"I'm gonna make breakfast," Cubby announced. "Would either of you bitches like Cap'n Crunch?"

I stifled a laugh. Tedd started to say, "Sugary cereals are..." and stopped himself. He was outnumbered. Cubby came back with three bowls of cereal and almond milk. He handed one to me and one to Tedd who looked at it and made a face.

I ate a big spoonful, "YUM! Isn't it delicious, Tedd? Don't you want to thank Cubby?"

Tedd swallowed with a gulp. He was never a swallower. "Thank you, Cubby," he said, sadly.

It didn't make me happy to see Tedd sad, but it didn't make me sad, either.

It did make me happy to write the alien script:

```
INT. SPACE SHIP - ENDLESS NIGHT (it's fucking
space!)

ZORN, 4,256,328.5 earth years old but looks good
for his age, like a 35 year old Brad Pitt, who's
considered a 4 out of 10 on Zorn's home planet of
ZzYzX. He lounges while his glowing white
spacecraft streams so well past light speed that
there's just a blur of colors. The ship has no
visible controls. It doesn't need them, it's
smart enough to cross dimensions in its sleep,
which it does.

Zorn looks at data floating in front of him.
Images speed by faster than the human eye can
comprehend, except in this case we do manage to
see smiling bikini clad women on pristine
beaches, "fitness model" men with 12-packs gym
mirror selfies, food porn, and other staples of
generally unrealistic Instagram feeds.

ZORN (Voice Over)
Holy scriptures of humanity. We study you to
learn what is important to this species, so
stupid that we must save your world from you.
```

In the background we see Norz, a glowing amorphous blob, zip herself into a human body container that looks like a Salma Hayak, age 35, so voluptuously form-fitting that even a gay screenwriter could be turned on by her.

NORZ

Does my butt look big in this body?

ZORN
Thankfully yes. I spent a full 3 seconds fighting with the matter adapter to shape that posterior. Someone on ZyZyX had programmed it to 1980 standards of beauty which were woefully out of date.

ZORN

David is writing me as if I am an intergalactic idiot. Yes, at first I found humanity confusing—because it is. It's difficult to understand a species that has swarmed over a planet and cannot see that the ultimate consequences of their actions are suicidal.

In David's case, he can't even see the consequences of his actions a few minutes ahead. He is the idiot. He thinks he invents his stories, but no, he merely opens his mind to the multi-dimensional story plane and they enter his head. That's how I got into his. I chose him, actually, because I knew he was already so consumed with his grief and libido that I could have my way with him, and I shall.

I also shall, as is my life's work, guide him to happiness, and foodstuffs that will cause him to shrink in size and emit less gas.

David was a fool to let Lu go. Being inside his head I know how his thought processes are warped through emotions. We have emotions, too, but so refined as to help us make *better* decisions, not worse ones as he does.

As he hears my voice grow stronger in my head, he will, at first, imagine this to be his own voice, or conscience. That's OK, whatever floats his boat. Yes, I know colloquialisms like that because they're inside his head. Also because we have boats on our planet, which are favored places to have sex. Actually, on our planet, everywhere is a favored place to have sex. On our planet, sex is the highest form of communion and communication. On this planet, David is just a horny idiot.

DAVID

I could hear Zorn's voice more clearly as I wrote. He was kind of an asshole, but of course any superior beings would be after having to deal with us. I mean, look at me, I was a horny idiot, enjoying Cubby's presence in my bed (on weekends only), and also enjoying that he annoyed Tedd.

Tedd was sleeping in the tiny "pool house" we had built thinking we'd build a pool but which I could never quite afford.

I was afraid to let Tedd back in the house because I might *accidentally* fuck him. It wouldn't have been on purpose, or sober, but it was going that direction when I got a text from Cubby: "Don't go there, girl!" For someone non-binary he sure liked to call me "Girl" a lot, which I didn't mind, because I did like wearing the kilt he made for me from a plaid sports coat I hadn't worn since Tedd gave it to me.

TEDD

I made David think I was miserable sleeping out here in what we laughingly referred to as the "Pool House." It was really more of a beautifully designed folly with a floor to ceiling glass wall and a 1920s Czech deco daybed. I designed and decorated this, so of course it was beautiful—and perfectly comfortable.

I couldn't sleep in the second bedroom because that was David's sacred writing space into which no mere mortal could trespass. That's what it said on the sign I had made for him and hung on his office door, "Let no mere mortals enter this sacred chamber." I meant it as a joke. He took it seriously. Even *Lady Clean*, our cleaning lady's legal name, wasn't allowed in. I haven't been in his office for years, so for all I knew he had a closet full of men in there. More likely M&Ms.

But, the thing was, I wouldn't have minded if he'd had a baker's dozen of men in there—good for him. He deserved it. He wasn't the world's best top, but he was a good guy. And sooner or later he'd realize it was good for me to have a few different men in my pool house because that was how modern relationships worked: We take care of ourselves first, then we take care of each other.

The truth is that David always took care of me. I know it, but I'd never have admitted it in the past. In the beginning, he bankrolled my clothing line, *Thredds*. Once it turned a profit I paid him back; still, he was the one who bought this house. He bought me my Jag, too. He was very generous.

I was sure I'd win him back because we'd always loved each other. In my case, just never exclusively.

ZORN

Tedd is an idiot, too.

LAWRENCE

I wasn't proud of this but I bought a drone with the express purpose of flying it over David's house to look in the back windows. I could see Tedd living in this small shed with glass walls. He masturbated a lot. I could see he and David were not really back together.

I could also see Cubby coming over on weekends. I had even had the drone hover outside the bedroom when they had sex. They were cute together. It was maddening.

Yasmin continued to seduce me successfully. Dory asked me if I thought I was bi, and I said given my sexual attraction to her (meaning Yasmin) the answer must be yes, but I also had a strong urge for dick. She laughed (meaning Dory). Dory didn't laugh much but it made me feel good to make her laugh. David must have felt good making so many people laugh.

I was sure I could get over David—in Wyoming.

YASMIN

Wyoming? What the actual fuck?

CUBBY

Being David's Weekend Boyfriend was perfect. I wasn't long out of a bad relationship with Elias, a non-binary, non-representational painter and my first long-term partner. It was Elias who helped me realize I was non-binary, too. Elias was 67 years old, their father was Hawaiian, their mother Finnish and they were nothing short of fabulous.

Elias's paintings made me taste colors. That was my first experience with synesthesia and it was addictive. Fuchsia was lime, periwinkle was salami, ruby was nachos. The colors in the painting didn't relate to the colors of the food, but the sense was so strong I felt like I was in another world.

It was intoxicating and beautiful, and started my appreciation of color that's the basis for my clothing line *Eat Me*. Tedd had a clothing line, too—trapped, as it was, in the patriarchal blinders of traditional masculinity. It also felt to me like warmed-over Ralph Lauren. Don't get me wrong, I love me some Ralphy. I found a pink (smelled to me like chocolate) cropped angora sweater at a thrift store that became one of my favorite pieces (I consider my belly button one of my best features and it was, in fact, featured on the cover of "NOM" magazine's spring "rebirth" issue).

Elias was a very jealous person. Possessive. Suffocating. Not literally, if they'd put their hands around my neck I might have broken theirs. But instead they put their psyche around mine and I didn't realize it until the colors in their paintings started tasting like bile.

I told Elias my mother was ill and I needed to fly back to Glendale to see her but that was a lie. I packed up all my stuff. "I may have to be there a while," I told Elias, and left. I did, in fact, stay with my mother and her silly-putty third husband, Mark, for two weeks until I found a commune of like minded people I could move in with.

I had the attic space entirely to myself, with a view of the treetops and a nest of goldfinches whose color tasted like asparagus.

I loved my little tree house. It was big enough for my bed, a work table, and bolts of fabric. I spent the week channeling a young Elsa Schiaparelli, creating deliciously colorful genderless clothes for all body shapes which I sold on Etsy.

I loved working during the week and fucking on the weekends.

DAVID

I liked to pamper Cubby. I used to do that for Tedd. It would make me feel... You know, I'd talked with Dory about it and never quite found the right word. "Useful" was too prosaic and shallow. "Fulfilled," was closer but no, my writing did that. "Connected?" Maybe that was it.

I liked making people happy. At least that was my intention. I learned from Dory that we can't "make" anyone else anything. You couldn't be sure that doing something you thought was nice for someone else would make them happy. Maybe they would resent you. Maybe it would hit a long-dormant nerve and make them miserable. There was no way to know. So giving was about giving, not about how it was received.

That was a big help for my writing, especially with *Stunning Aliens*, because I wasn't trying to manipulate the audience, or the characters. I was letting it *unfold*.

ZORN

David thinks he came to the "unfolding" realization on his own. Ha! Humans are funny. Mostly dumb, but still funny. We have an entire wavelength on ZzYzX devoted to watching humans. The most popular programs are the "orgasm faces" which we find hilarious, but pretty much everything humans do is either disgustingly stupid or hilarious. Often both at the same time as far as we are concerned.

DAVID

I was a little bit concerned at hearing Zorn's voice even when I wasn't writing. Like when I'd be cumming inside of Cubby, I'd hear alien giggling coming from somewhere inside my head.

But it was good he was taking on a life of own as a character. And I understood the giggling, Cubby made funny faces when they climaxed.

Cubby was a doll—a life-sized doll. I sometimes had to remind myself that they were human, especially since I called them *they* which in my mind had more distance than *he*.

Cubby and I fit together. So why did I still think about Lu?

CUBBY

David called me *Lu* by accident. At first I was shocked. It'd been months since either of us had seen Lu who had moved to Cheyenne with Cheyenne. Every time I thought about that it would make me giggle. Not just the Cheyenne part, but Lu had always seemed like *London* and there he was in Laramie. What could he possibly be doing there? Panning for gold?

Wyoming had a lot of rocks. Maybe he was collecting them the way I collected fabric when I apprenticed with Donatella. God she was weird. I knew it was just plastic surgery, but one night I dreamed that she performed human sacrifices to keep herself looking young-adjacent. I couldn't risk sticking around after that and told her my mother was sick. That was always my excuse and it was true. My mother was always sick— bipolar (though I liked to say the correct medical term was "nutjob.") Mark, her poor blob of a husband, had no idea what he was getting into, and might never have figured it out because he smoked so much pot. He got her on it, which frankly, made her a lot happier.

I was distracting myself from parsing the fact that David called me Lu. These things happened. Though I never called him *Elias*. Or Betty. Or Tremaine. Or Gabby. Or Mopsy.

I'd loved them all, deeply if briefly, and now I loved David. I was not flighty, I was a glorious phoenix, constantly reborn to fly.

LAWRENCE

Cheyenne. The place and the face. Both surprisingly sexy.

I couldn't wait to leave. Both.

I loved the geological formations. I loved the Wyoming Jade, "the most famous of the state's geologic treasures," as the brochures read. I met with miners and amassed a collection of native Wyoming diamonds, sapphires, opal, peridot and quartz crystals. Even some pretty petrified wood.

I went to rodeos and watched Cheyenne ride the backs of unhappy bulls while bedraggled clowns pulled him away from what looked to me like near certain death.

It was the kind of "wild west" thing I remember loving in movies when I was a kid. David wrote a movie called "Yosemite Kid," about an orphan who finds his way to Yosemite and is raised by a "mama bear" named Charmaine. In a surprising twist, it was revealed Charmaine was actually a park ranger in a bear suit. At the time this was sold as silly rather than what I now knew it to be: a "furry" or sexual kink of people who like dressing up as animals.

When my mother would make me participate in sports I would say to her, "If you were Charmaine you'd never do this to me!" Finally she said, "Who is this

Charmaine creature," and I said, "Exactly, she's a creature, a bear in this funny movie." We watched it together and laughed together. That's what David's movies did, brought people closer together.

She finally asked me, "OK, baby, what would Charmaine make you do?" and I said ballroom dancing and my mama bear got me ballroom dancing lessons. My partner and I, Bibi, were world champion cha cha dancers in the age 12-14 group. My mother still has my sparkly costume in a cedar closet.

So, there I was in the Wild West. Cheyenne couldn't have been happier. He'd introduce me to his cowboy friends and I could barely understand a word they said. I heard one of them say to him, "I caint unnerstan a word yer boyfrund shez."

I thought a boxful of rocks and gemstones could keep me grounded. I was wrong.

YASMIN

I'd had fun buying a wardrobe for Montana. Wyoming. Whatever. Suede with fringe and gold studs. Knee-high alligator fuck-me boots. Lawrence had his fun in and with Cheyenne. Or was it "in and in Cheyenne." Didn't matter. It was time for him to stop playing cowboy and come home and play husband.

"Why didn't you meet me at the airport?" I fumed when I got to his... bus.

"I thought you were joking, I didn't think you'd actually come," he said. "But it's good to see you."

He was very tan, which I liked, and felt more buff, which was hot. "I lift a lot of rocks and here we mostly eat buffalo." Whatever it was, it worked for him.

"Time to come home, Lufti." I only called him "Lufti" because I knew it was what his mama called him and thought it would get under his skin. All's fair in love and war.

"OK" he said. Just like that.

He packed his suitcase, wrote a little note to Cheyenne and left with me to the airport in a terrible dusty taxi that was only one step up from a donkey.

CHEYENNE

"Dear Cheyenne, I'm sorry, but I must go back to Los Angeles. You have been a dear to me, but I have seen how that clown, Shep, looks at you and I won't stand in the way. Love, Lawrence."

Shep had such a thing for me that he made his 3-foot clown boner a part of his act, somehow always pointing at me. He and I would chew the cud and drink beer and bandage each other's wounds.

I felt a little bad, because I thought Larry was head over heels about me, having never met a real man before. But Shep was more of a real man than Larry, and I figured he'd get over me when he got back to LA.

I sent a text to him when he landed in LAX. "Dear Larry. Thanks for being a hero and stepping aside for Shep. We'll always have a cot for you in our bus. Your friend, Benny."

LAWRENCE

It made me a little sad. But not as sad as Yasmin handing me a key to her condo and hearing myself say, "I really need to focus on my dissertation so I can only see you on weekends."

What the fuck had I just said???

Holy freaking mother of diamond-encrusted fuck!

Now I knew exactly how David felt. Except in my case, I also wanted to avoid spending too much time with Yas. Then I had to wonder if David wanted to avoid spending too much time with me, too.

I had a double session with Dory talking about this. Was I like Yas?? Obnoxious? Pushy? Bitchy? Unrealistic? Heterosexual? Dory talked me down, in that breathy way of hers. Even when my head was pounding with negative self-talk, it was always relaxing to watch her perfectly coiffed hair bounce as she spoke.

"Let's break this down because there are two issues happening simultaneously and you don't want to confuse them. One is realizing that a person can need time and space to focus on their work passion vs personal passion. In your case, the other is that you have expressed clearly that you want Yasmin to be your friend, not your girlfriend."

She made things seem so simple.

I did not tell her I wanted David back. I saved that information for Yasmin. And Cubby.

YASMIN

FUCK! What does David have that I don't, other than a dick?

"I bought a strap-on while you were away!" I screamed, running back from the bedroom with it in my hands. It was an 8" translucent and sparkly pink dildo mounted on a pink patent leather harness.

Boo recoiled. I don't know if I'd ever even thought of the word "recoil" before, but he totally did it.

"That thing is massive!," he cried, actual tears forming in his sweet brown eyes.

"I only bought it because I thought you'd like it! I can get a smaller one. They also come in teal!" I cried, too. Now we were both crying though I kind of forgot who was crying about what.

"I love you, Yas. I always have and I always will. But I can't marry you. You know that."

"I don't know that. We could have a very postmodern marriage like Diane Von Furstenberg and Barry Diller. You can fuck your boyfriends and I can fuck them, too!"

I saw the corners of his mouth inch upward, then he pursed his lips trying not to laugh, and failing. "You're a hoot, I love you," he laughed in my ear.

"I know," I laughed back, close to his ear, purposely a little too loud because I wanted to punish him.

He picked up the strap-on. "Do you even know how to use this thing?"

"No, but I figured if all else failed I could remove the dildo part and wear it as a cute belt."

"That would be cute," he agreed.

We tried it that way. It was.

CUBBY

"I want David back," Lawrence texted me out of the blue. Not "Hello" not "How are you doing?" Not "How's all the burgundy taffeta you bought working out for you?" Nope, just "I want David back."

I texted him back, "That's too bad, bub."

It's not that I was a possessive person by any stretch of the imagination. In fact, I felt my time was running out with David, not because he was boring or anything, in fact, he knew just how to make me laugh.

One of my favorite things was when he'd make up stories about my cock, which he named Taylor.

"Taylor is having a moment," he said, sticking little googly eyes on the head and taking closeup pics. "They were shopping at Bonwits..." (I had to ask him what a Bonwit was and it turned out to be some ancient department store from before I was born) "...when they discovered they only sold tighty whities!"

The combination of the wistful look on Taylor's tiny face and the term "tighty whitey" made me giggle. I hated that kind of underwear. It didn't look good on anyone, even supermodels. It was made only for actual jockeys and little boys and nobody else should have ever worn it. Ever. Unless it was on their head like a hat.

I made a silkscreen print of Taylor and put it on a series of upcycled t-shirts from the Goodwill. They sold like hotcakes to Midwestern Republican ladies who just thought it was a funny face and had no idea what it actually was. Hil-ar-i-ous.

Then I got the letter from Elias's lawyer. I was afraid to open it.

ZORN
I put David in the trance and wrote 26 pages of effervescent comedy gold. It was only upon writing the

button to a particularly madcap scene that I realized I'd been writing it in my native language rather than English.

I was so shocked that David snapped out of a trance. When he saw what he considered to be gibberish he was so upset he deleted it, then spent 45 minutes with tech support who told him to reinstall the software.

DAVID

Cubby said, "Put this under your tongue" so I did. I saw stars. I saw planets. I saw colors and lights and was pretty sure Taylor was talking to me and Zorn had taken over my brain. It was fun.

It took six hours to come back to reality. I found 26 pages of gibberish in my screenplay, starting with "Coke dwight sweater-set peanut glucose shamrock mother-of-pearl dongle..." and ending with "<<GdTvZeZeZeZ>> [YxYxYxYx] {ZyZyZyXxZ}"

I spent 45 minutes on the phone with tech support who didn't believe me when I told them my brain had been hijacked.

ZORN

Nobody had the heart to tell Tedd that he was looking puffy these days, so I took it upon myself to use David's mouth to tell him. I hope I was speaking English.

TEDD

Fat? Me? David didn't seem quite himself but I understood him loud and clear.

I took off all my clothes and stood in front of the glossy black refrigerator because David wouldn't allow me in the master bath to use the only full-length mirror in the house. It was then I knew I'd made a horrible mistake four years ago—I should have ordered the brushed stainless steel French door Sub-Zero so I wouldn't have to see my hideous reflection today.

I quickly covered my quivering flesh with camouflage pattern sweats and drove to the gym where I worked my ass off until I felt faint.

I would be having no more gentleman callers over until I whipped myself back into shape and wondered if the ones who had seen me this way were telling their friends.

Em-bare-assed doesn't even begin to describe it.

SHELLI

"I have kept my mouth shut for everything except my regular truffled filets but I can stay silent no longer," I said, spooning muskmelon gelato I flew in from Rome into his mouth. This was necessary when I had anything remotely painful or even honest to tell him. I learned, though multiple husbands, that this was the only way to 1) get a man's attention, and 2) soften the blow (other than a blow job, and frankly I find it hard to blow and speak at the same time, plus my knees are not they once were when I won "Miss Sandusky, Ohio 1968," so Roman gelato was just a lot easier.

David made some noise as if he was going to say something, so I gently shoved another spoonful into his mouth.

"You have got to get Tedd out of your house."

David grabbed the spoon and pushed it into my mouth. "He's *not* living in my house, Shell, he's living in the folly in the backyard."

I extracted said spoon, only after having taken the time to let the unique heritage melon taste and aroma waft into my recently cleansed sinuses. "You mean the glorified tool shed? I don't care, it's still too close for comfort. Why are you being such a pushover?" I asked, using the most loving tone I could manage with a brain freeze.

"You don't have to worry, Shell, he's not allowed in my bedroom and can only use the kitchen on odd-numbered hours so we won't run into each other."

I smacked him in the face with the gelato and let it run down his chin. This is where "Poofter," my poodle, came in handy, licking up food before it became a mess that my butler/lover, Hiroto, would have to deal with. I kissed his forehead, "I'm saying this with love, but you're an idiot."

"I've been hearing that word in my head a lot lately," he admitted to me, which I thought was sweet, as it's not often that men admit to their stupidity.

"Cubby is with me on weekends," he said in lieu of an explanation. I met Cubby and they were adorable. I'd sometimes find the two skinny dipping in one of my three pools, which I didn't mind but the gardeners complained about.

"He's not with you during the week, and that's when I worry," I explained. Having run out of the gelato I rang for Hiroto to bring a full English tea.

"I love it that you worry, love," he said, kissing me on the cheek. "But I've got it all under control." He smiled that cute smile of his and I made the gagging noise I make when I don't believe someone, or when they say "American Cheese."

"You don't owe him anything, David. It's not like Jez was his first indiscretion." He looked confused, surprised, quizzical and just the tiniest bit stupid. He wasn't dumb, but could he possibly have not known about Tedd's extracurricular activities?

"What" was all he could manage to say.

"Are you playing dumb or actually dumb?" I asked him, again, with love. "I never said anything because I thought you must obviously know and because he always came back to you, at least until you threw him out."

"Uhhh."

"Look, honey, you're being dense. You need to get that creature out of your house before he worms his way back into your bed."

"Naw..." At this point I wondered if he'd literally been struck dumb.

"Yaw. I saw you two go at it on my boccie court that night two years ago when you both thought I was in Sweden but I was actually taking a staycation in my east wing. You boys fucked like bunnies and that was after 15 years of marriage."

"You were…" he only managed to form two words.

"Look, I understand. My third and fourth husband Syd and I were insatiable. In bed, in the limo, in the Gulfstream jet, in his mother's powder room, in our private box at the opera. You name it, we did it. That's why I didn't notice when he was transferring funds to his private Swiss bank account. If it hadn't been for Monsieur Müeller at the Swiss National Bank I never would have noticed because I was too busy orgasming. This is why I am warning you. Now, where's that tea?"

Luckily Hiroto arrived with the tea service: Russ & Daughters cheese sandwiches (I despised cucumbers except when disguised as dill pickles), scones, clotted cream, jam, meringues, macarons, and the marzipan petit fours that David always favored. I stuffed a petit four into his mouth so he wouldn't even attempt to speak.

"Kick him out on his ass, even though it's always been one of his best features."

David swallowed with a gulp and took my hand in both of his. "Shell, I love love love you. You know that. But I'm a grown-ass man and I know what I'm doing."

"When men call themselves 'grown-ass' they rarely know what they're doing, dear. But it's your life. If you want to ruin it with Tedd then all I ask is that you don't come crying back to me, by which I mean of course you must come crying back to me, but that at some point in the parlay that follows I will have to say 'I told you so,' and you'll have to say 'Yes, you did warn me, you gorgeous creature, you,' then all will be forgiven." I had to take a deep breath because that was a very long sentence.

"You gorgeous creature," he said, sweetly before downing another petit four. Oh, I'd forgotten to give him tea and was afraid he'd choke so I quickly poured it and gestured for him to drink up as Hiroto always made it the perfect temperature that required no cooling.

"Now I must go. I am late for my pelvic floor exercise class with Señor Velasquez. He has the most marvelous hairline. Ta-ta, my love!"

DAVID

I was so lucky to have a friend like Shell, and I knew she meant well, but I *was* a grown-ass man and I could deal with Tedd. The weird thing was, now that he'd put on a few pounds he was actually even more attractive to me, more of a bear than an otter, and I'd find myself sneaking looks at him when he showered in the folly's outdoor shower. Damn.

But now, with nothing sweet in my mouth to distract me, I thought about what Shell said about Tedd's extracurricular activities. I always assumed that was the case, but we had a kind of don't-ask-don't-tell arrangement which I never actually asked about. I'd never cheated, but then I don't consider making out, oral and/or frottage cheating.

Oh, saying that reminded me of Lu, because we had "asked and told" about that and agreed.

Lu. I liked his brain. I liked his body. I liked his accent. I liked his skin, his teeth and his eyes. His kindness and creativity. When he was in the throes of climax he didn't make funny faces, he looked serene like I was fucking a fucking God.

He laughed at all my jokes. Even the ones I didn't think were funny, he thought were funny. He had a beautiful laugh and those beautiful teeth.

He smelled like the ocean and when I put my ear to his ear I could hear the ocean, too! Whoosh. Whoosh. Sigh.

I guessed he was still in Cheyenne. With Cheyenne. I'd been a fool to let him go. It was a Wednesday, so I jerked off thinking about Lu and it was so good I had to wipe off my chin afterwards.

CUBBY

The lawyer's letter said that Elias had died and left me his house in Kauai which he named Māhū, Hawaiian for "third gender." The will stipulated that I was to commission a sculptor to create a 12' high statue of Elias's erect phallus, and that it be spouting an "eternal flame" at the tip. He'd left detailed drawings. And photographs.

The will ended, "I hope your mother is feeling better" and was dated six years ago, so he must have written it thinking I was coming back and never bothered to change it. Or, maybe, under all his insane jealousy and possessiveness, he actually loved me.

I cried for three days. Partly because I was so deeply touched and partly because I now owned real estate, something I didn't think would happen in my lifetime.

A plan immediately sprang to mind: I would create "the Māhū retreat for non-binary makers and artists." We would have monthly salons for the locals and international art critics and make Kauai like Paris in the 20s.

DAVID

Cubby didn't show up that weekend. I texted him... 27 times and got no answer. I was worried something had happened to him.

DORY

Twenty-seven times. You would think he'd have figured it out after, say, seventeen, but no.

One of the frustrating things about being a therapist was that other people's problems were obvious—to me, at least—not to them. Then again, it was always easier to see someone else's problems than my own.

Not to mention that their problems felt more valuable because they paid me to listen to them.

Nobody paid me to listen to myself, so how much could my issues be worth? Nothing. Except when I told them to my therapist, Selma, at which point I was paying her, so my problems had value again.

Selma said, "Your issues are just as valid as your patient's, just as mine are just as valid as yours." Selma had it all together, which is why she charged twice as much as I did.

TEDD

Cubby didn't show up so I seized the opportunity.

I stuck my head in while Davey was making stuffed pasta shell enchiladas. "That smells delicious, Davey."

"It's your lucky day, Teddo, I have extra," he said, forlorn.

"Where's your adorable friend, Cubby?" I asked, innocently enough, even though I knew full well he wasn't there.

"Um, he's..." Davey started. I could immediately tell he was lying because he never said *Um* and actively mocked people who said it. "He's... um... away?"

"Mind if I come in?" I slipped through the sliding glass door even before he answered.

"Sure, I'll make you a plate." He was always such a good cook it was surprising I didn't get fat before, but my first trainer trained me to be bulimic, then I started taking Ritalin because I'd heard it was really an amphetamine like my mother took as diet pills and I could get them legally from Dr. Southwark.

Davey handed me a plate literally overflowing with food.

"Too much, I've put on weight and feel like a pig," I told him.

"It suits you." he said with a smile. I couldn't tell if that was sincere or snark.

What I said next wasn't calculated, it was honest, "You have always been such a sweet man, that's why I love you." I took a bite of the pasta shell, filled with refried beans, taco meat and an ambrosial guacamole/sour cream substance, all covered in a mole sauce. "This dish is genius, babe." The word *babe* just came out the way it used to.

We ate in silence but I saw him eyeing me. I stopped eating before I had too much because I was watching my weight, and because if I was going to seduce him, it couldn't be on a full stomach as then there'd be a lot of decidedly unsexy sloshing.

"I miss you so much," I said, which *was* calculated, but I did miss him, too. We used to have the perfect relationship. I could fuck around and still come home to a cute, successful husband. I didn't appreciate it, but now I do.

"I miss what we had," Davey said, sadly. "But..."

I didn't let him continue, "...We can have it again, babe. Things will be different this time."

I noticed his eyebrows twitch, which happened when he heard a line of dialog he didn't like, like when I'd mistakenly said, "This isn't how it looks" with Jez. I wondered if I'd taken that line from a bad TV movie. "I know I was a fool— I've learned my lesson."

No eyebrow twitches. I leaned in and kissed him. He was always a good kisser. A better kisser than a top, but sometimes that's all you really want, like when you've had a long day and want to go to sleep and you don't really want Jez prodding his 8" in your face...

It was a delicious kiss, a combination of Davey and MexItalian food. I probed my tongue deeper into his mouth, something that always made him melt.

Then I took his hand and led him into the bedroom. "I love you," I said, feeling it.

The passion was palpable. And he'd learned a few tricks from his boyfriends. The flat tongue blow job move was epic, and I maybe it was hate-fucking but damn, it was good.

He fell right to sleep as he always did after sex. I looked at his face in the moonlight. A little round in a way I could tell myself was "boyish." But a good man. Too good for me, probably, but I wasn't going to let that stop me.

DAVID

I woke up with the sun reflecting off my face, making Tedd literally glow. Shit, he was handsome. Fuck, he was good in bed. And he said he loved me.

What the fuckity fuck did I do?

DORY

What the fuck did he do? We'd discussed Tedd and how backsliding into his backside was not going to bring back the past. I spoke from experience, remembering that time when I let my ex, Ronan back into my life... and bed.

Needless to say it didn't turn out well, which is an understatement. He was gone the next morning, along with my late grandmother's pearl necklace, my laptop, and my pride. It was only later that I found the empty bottle of Rohypnol in the bathroom trash and realized Ronan had roofied me.

I asked my father's best friend, Georgio, who talked like one of the guys in "The Godfather," to break Ronan's legs. It didn't happen because it turned out Georgio was just a pastry chef. If only Ronan had been a diabetic...

LAWRENCE

Fuck it, I was just going to knock on Davey's door. It was Monday, so he'd be alone and I'd tell him I was sorry and I'd be happy to be his weekend boyfriend.

Yasmin said, "Don't grovel, it's not at all attractive."

"I'm not groveling, I'm just..."

"What?" she prodded me with her shiny red fingernail.

"OK, I'm groveling."

"Aha!" she cried, mostly because her nail got caught in the button hole of my jacket and broke while she was angrily yanking it out.

"Can you honestly tell me you've never groveled?" I asked her.

"I don't grovel. I give head" she said, regally.

"Good idea, I'll try that," I said as I left and heard her calling her manicurist.

I knocked on David's door and waited nervously. The door opened. It was Tedd. Naked.

Shitty shit shit.

"What?" he said.

"Is David..."

He slammed the door in my face.

DAVID

"Who was that at the door?" I asked Tedd, who'd answered it completely naked. If I'd looked like him I'd be naked in the frozen food department at Pavilions supermarket.

"Mormons," he said, turning around, his dick swinging.

"I'd love some of your pita pancakes," he said, lounging on the sofa in a pose that looked both casually sensual and studied.

"Good idea, I haven't made them in a while, Cubby was gluten intoler..." I stopped mid-sentence. I still hadn't heard from Cubby. For a moment my writer's mind wondered if Tedd had him killed. But Tedd wasn't a murderer, just an adulterer. I could accept that, though I would have to draw the line at murder. I can say that with full moral certainty. "Tell me the truth, Tedd, do you know what happened to Cubby?"

He sat up without using his hands. Even with the few extra pounds he looked good in a sitting position. "No, babe, sorry I don't. It does seem awfully rude of him just to disappear like that."

Wasn't that what a murderer would say? "You didn't happen to murder him, did you?" I asked, thinking I'd catch him off-guard.

"Nope. I'd never do that. Sounds messy and unpleasant."

Now I knew he was telling the truth because he was never interested in anything messy or unpleasant, even in bed.

The first pita pancakes were a tad soggy because I was out of practice, but I ate those and made another crispier batch for Tedd, like I always used to do. It was so easy to fall back into our old pattern.

Later that day Tedd moved his "TrimLine" boxer briefs into my dresser drawer. Those were the first of his underwear designs and had caught the attention of an editor at GQ and started Tedd's career. I'd come up with the name "Trimline" from the old telephones. I joked it was either that or "princess" but he didn't get it— there were princess phones and Trimline phones... oh, never mind, it's not a joke if you have to explain it.

ZORN

Tedd was very good at sex. I experienced it all from inside David's brain where the neurons were firing so fast it approached the mental acuity of one of our newly born beings. Normally human brains were slower than one of our unborn globules, already learning 6 languages, as well as advanced calculus in their chrysalis.

Experiencing sex firsthand was an important learning opportunity for me. Our kind procreated by merging our entire beings together, then dropping energetic particles which would be grown into new beings.

Norz and I had watched much sexual research during our journey and learned the importance of making animal noises and saying "fuck," but having experienced this bizarre mating ritual from inside an actual human body was enlightening.

I transmitted what I had learned to Norz so they would also be skilled in the art of sex.

I felt sorry for David. Being inside his mind I felt what he felt and he was so eager to go back to life as it was before someone called Jez. He longed for the familiar repetitive patterns of Tedd.

I could read Tedd's mind, too, and he was not to be trusted. He loved David in his own way, which is to say selfish if slightly sincere. He looked more like the humans in our research materials from xHamster and PornTube than David did. He was also very good at the animal noises and saying "fuck" like he really meant it.

He was genuinely surprised by David's performance and enjoyed it, but in the middle he was thinking about pancakes.

SHELLI

I had a sixth sense about these things. It was 1 am. Hiroto had just gotten out of my bed and I had this feeling that David had succumbed to Tedd. I didn't call that night because I might as well let him enjoy the night together as I enjoyed the night alone in my double-king-sized heart-shaped bed.

Tedd was nothing if not selfish, but in the past I had found selfish lovers to be a wonderful challenge. "What can I do to make him actually notice that there's another human being naked beside him?"

David is nothing if not a people-pleaser, so his neuroses meshed with Tedd's like the gears in my diamond encrusted Philippe

Patek Golden Compass wristwatch. Only in their case, the ticking was that of a time bomb.

The next morning I sent Hiroto in the Rolls to pick up David.

"Luckily I answered the door," David told me.

"If it was Tedd it wouldn't have been anything Hiroto hadn't seen before," I informed him.

DAVID

Hiroto, too? Well, yes, I could understand why. Hiro was beautiful, had impeccable manners and was a Le Cordon Bleu trained pastry chef as well. I'd eat petit fours off his naked ass.

"You were right," I told Shelli.

SHELLI

"I told you so," I replied as I'd told him I would. "And?"

"You gorgeous creature, you," he added, correctly.

"And now we shall move on" I said, magnanimously because if he genuinely wanted to go back to Tedd then who was I to judge after having married Syd twice.

"I just wish I knew what happened to Cubby," he sighed.

"What was his last name?"

"Smith. But he went by *Cadillac*."

I tapped this into my phone. "This may take a few minutes," I informed him. "Why don't you go skinny dipping with Hiroto, I do enjoy watching you boys do swan dives."

David dropped his clothes and dove into the pool. I watched Hiroto emerge from the deep end holding a silver tray with petit fours—the man was a culinary genius and a sensitive lover. I'd be lost without him.

When most people thought of me, as they did often, they thought of my fabulous sense of style, my stunning generosity, and my perfect breasts (they were mine, I paid for them). But only my closest friends also knew of my cutting wit, razor-sharp business acumen, and command of technology.

I saw the internet as an extension of myself and connection to humanity, whether it was finding the perfect artisanal necklace, working towards a more efficient yet humane organizational system or finding anyone, anywhere, anytime. So I would find Cubby for David.

I was distracted by a series of text messages and by the time I looked up, I saw Hiroto lying face down on the grass while David nibbled petit fours off his ass. Why had I never thought to do this?

"Yoo hoo!" I called out to him. "I hate to interrupt such a delightful repast, but I have news for you about Cubby. I watched David offer thanks to Hiroto with a kiss on his ass. Then he wrapped himself in a custom made Turkish towel with my crest and stepped inside.

"Cubby's in Kauai. He inherited a house from his former lover, Elias. His phone was swallowed by a giant sea turtle and he lost his contacts. Here's his new number from T-mobile," I told him.

"You're a wonder, Shell." David said, gratefully.

"And?" I asked.

"A fucking gorgeous creature."

"Thank you, dear. And thank you for teaching Hiroto a new trick."

He dressed and gave me a kiss before he left.

"Hiroto, are there any petit fours left?"

He replied huskily, "Yes, you gorgeous creature!"

HIROTO

PETIT FOURS WERE A PAIN IN THE ASS TO MAKE. BUT TODAY THEY WERE WORTH IT. DAVID'S BEARD TICKLING MY ASS GAVE ME GOOSEBUMPS ALL OVER.

ALSO, WHILE SHELLI WAS A SURPRISINGLY LIMBER LOVER GIVEN HER AGE, SHE WAS ALSO DAMNED NEAR INSATIABLE AND AT 45 I WASN'T GETTING ANY YOUNGER.

SO IT WAS AT TIMES LIKE THIS, WHEN I DIDN'T FEEL LIKE BEING SMOTHERED BY HER IMPRESSIVE BREASTS IN MY FACE, THAT IT WAS MUCH MORE RELAXING TO FEEL HER NIBBLING MY ASS.

DAVID

Now I understood why I'd been so prolific when I was with Tedd. On one hand, I loved him and was happy. But there was always this underlying sense that I wasn't good enough for him that made me miserable. Now I see I was *too good* for him, which makes me miserable so my writing is progressing nicely.

```
INT. HOLIDAY INN, GROVERS MILL, CA - NIGHT

An unearthly glow emanates from the second floor
window of room 222. We see the silhouettes of two
perfect human specimens kissing, then humping
while we hear animal sounds including a goat,
chicken and screaming howler monkey.

                    ZORN
          FUCKITY FUCK FUCK

                    NORZ
              Meow!

CUT TO:

EXT. STRAWBERRY FIELD, GROVERS MILL, CA - DAY

Jack West, 50, a rugged farmer who looks 35,
drives his tractor through the field, plowing. It
stops with a crash, digging up the corner of a
spaceship.
```

NORZ

The concept of gender is alien to us. Zorn understands it better because he was previously on earth 400,000 years ago, so was used to wearing a human body.

But for us, a physical presence is cumbersome and limited when opposed to being a purely energetic being.

Zorn has taken the form of the male of the species. They said they did this because they already knew how to manipulate this kind of body. Having read the latest in human political discourse, I claimed this was Patriarchal Bullshit. Zorn laughed and said I was being silly and needed some time in a human brain, so he's giving me space in David's head.

David met a creature called Shelli. He was not physically attracted to her, perhaps because she was no longer of breeding age and would not be useful to our DNA repair project.

But he was interested in Hiroto, or at least in consuming sweets from his buttocks. This was not a practice of which we were previously aware and has been added to our list of modern human social interaction protocols.

YASMIN

Of course Boo came to me. "David's ex has a big dick!" he cried, not something I'd ever cried about, ever, not even when my exes, like Bruno, had one.

I gave Boo a piece of my beautiful mind, "They look nice swinging around, but they're a pain in the ass. And everywhere else. I mean, once you get past 6" what're you going to do with the rest of that thing? Choke on it? No thank you. Yours is the perfect size."

"You don't have to say that," he said, basically asking me to say it again.

"It's true. Yours fits everywhere I want it to be." I fanned myself like a beauty queen. "Besides, you told me David doesn't have a big dick…"

"…I didn't say that, I wouldn't have said that, when did I say that? And yes it's true."

Why did I have to bring up David? I'm just too nice, that's what it is. Too nice for my own good. I thought about playing up Tedd's size to make Boo feel bad, but damn my intrinsic goodness, I couldn't do it!

Also, due to my intrinsic goodness, I felt it wise to remove my IUD. It seemed very wrong to deprive the world of the exquisite children that Boo and I could create. Seriously, it would have been sad never to see their beautiful little faces and YSL baby clothes. Not to mention downright tragic for poor Boo to never experience fatherhood and the associated marriage to me.

"It's OK, baby," I said, running my hand down the front of his pants. I was once again delighted to get an immediate response which led to sliding my hand down inside his pants to wrap around his perfectly sized cock.

He gave in. Men are so easy.

ZORN

David gave in to Tedd. Earth men are so easy. I watched, in horror, like a slow-mo car crash because my ability to project into the future made it clear to me that this would end in tears. Unfortunately, my future vision doesn't tell me *whose* tears.

DAVID

While I'm happy things are back to normal with Tedd, I can't help feeling that this will end in tears.

ZORN

Just then I felt a sharp pain in the area where a stomach would be if I had one. It was an alert from my ship— it had been disturbed. This could only mean one of two things: 1) That it hadn't buried itself deeply enough or maybe it did but got curious about the world above ground and was crawling out to take a look or 2) Someone was trying to steal it.

I couldn't even remember how many times space pirates tried to steal my sweet ride. Oh, that's right, I never forget anything. 12. And that was just in the past 400,000 years since I'd previously been on Earth!

Humans had hardly changed from the Neanderthals— they were still dumb, especially when they were horny.

Unfortunately, the DNA updating we did on the Neanderthals got diluted by Homo sapiens, so we would need to mate with many thousands of humans this time to complete the DNA revision. It was a dirty job, but somebody had to do it.

TEDD

I didn't know what had gotten into David. Whatever it was, I liked it.

He had an alien look in his eyes as he pushed me down on the sofa and hoarsely whispered he was going to give me an anal probe.

ZORN

Fuck yes!

DAVID

I didn't know what had gotten into me but I was aggressive and dominant with Tedd. I was going to show him who's boss—and did, repeatedly.

I also didn't know why my orgasm noises sounded like mooing.

Whatever it was, he liked it.

LAWRENCE

Yasmin was aggressive. I liked it.

I woke up to find myself in bed with her. She even looked pretty in the morning, though she snored like a lioness.

I was still confused as to how this happened. I felt bad about David, and Tedd... and Yasmin was so nice and understanding and sweet.

I wondered what *Y-Essel* meant when she yelled it during her climax. She said it was ancient Aramaic for "fuck!"

That was nice.

I wasn't oblivious to what she was trying to do—make me think that I was straight. But if I was straight would I like the small glittery teal strap-on dildo she fucked me with? She said, 'Straight men like it up the ass, too, you know.'"

I didn't. I googled it. It's true. Who knew?

DAVID

INT. MALE STRIP CLUB - LATE NIGHT

A bachelorette party. The women are wearing stupid shiny hats and waving penis shaped noisemakers.

Zorn is an exceptionally good exotic dancer, having studied tens of thousands of hours worth of video of sexy moves.

It also helps that he has the power to hypnotize. As he moves, we see the woman in the audience go into a trance and start taking off their own clothes.

SUPER SPEED MOTION

In about a minute of screen time we see Zorn mate with over 40 women.

INT. FEMALE STRIP CLUB - SAME TIME

The audience at a bachelor party. They are visibly wasted, bleary-eyed, half asleep.

Norz is also an exceptional dancer with the ability to hypnotize and soon the men start taking off their clothes.

SUPER SPEED MOTION

Again, in about a minute of screen time, we see her mate with at least 40 men.

INT. ZORN AND NORZ'S LOFT APARTMENT - DAWN

Everything in the apartment is shiny white, from
the ceiling, through the lacquered patent leather
furniture to the glossy floor.

                    ZORN
          I had an effective night,
          planting my altered DNA into
          forty women.

                    NORZ
          I was also effective, with 40
          men.

                    ZORN
          What? Men cannot receive our
          DNA?

Norz pulls out a strap-on.

                    NORZ
          They did—with this.

It shoots like a confetti cannon.

                    NORZ (Cont.)
          And they liked it!

Norz reaches down and drags an unconscious naked
male body across the shiny white floor.

                    ZORN
          What are you doing with that?

                    NORZ
          I was only going to eat this
          one.

                    ZORN
          You drop that right this minute,
          missy!

Norz looks sad. Picks up the body with ease and
tosses it out the window.

ZORN

On my planet I am known as a fine storyteller. I can project my vision directly into the sensate spheres of my species. I entertained them for millennia with tales of my first trip to this planet. After 10,000 years, though, the stories began to lose their erotic appeal.

Norz assumed my mantle of galactic storyteller after her excursion to a planet of sexually promiscuous cannibals, and even I had to admit she had something there.

This is why I asked her to accompany me on this mission. Now both of us will have tales to tell for eternity.

Of course, some of the tales take far more explanation than the actual story itself. One example is the "strip club" of which there is no equivalent on ZyZyX as we have no need for clothing, so there is no comprehension of the term.

Still, it was an entertaining escapade and will make an amusing anecdote.

TEDD

Things were good at home. So good I was already bored. Not entirely, just enough to make me look elsewhere. I felt no guilt or shame around my physical needs. This is what physical beings need.

David kept droning on about this script he was writing about aliens with no bodies.

"How do you write a sex movie without bodies?" I asked him, confused and more than a little worried he'd thrown away his clean comedy revenue stream for an untested future in adult entertainment.

"They zip on beautiful bodies, like Brad Pitt's. And I'm not writing porn. I'm writing a sex comedy."

Blah blah blah. I did like Brad Pitt. Well, the younger Brad. The older Pitt was too much like me, meaning extremely handsome in a mature way but not up to the level of perfection we once had. I had been perfect. Sometimes I'd beat off looking at old photos of myself.

Who wouldn't?

HIROTO

TEDD TOLD ME HE AND MR. DAVID HAD AN OPEN RELATIONSHIP NOW, WHICH WAS NOT A SURPRISE SINCE I'D SEEN MR. DAVID WITH LAWRENCE AND CUBBY.

WHILE TEDD COULD BE FUN, I SURE AS FUCK WASN'T GOING TO MAKE PETIT FOURS FOR HIM.

IN FACT, WHEN HE FLIRTED WITH ME I SAID, "I'M GAME, BUT YOU HAVE TO DO THE HARD WORK."

I LAY BACK AND ENJOYED IT, THOUGH IT STILL FELT LIKE WORK.

NONE OF THIS WAS PART OF MY JOB DESCRIPTION. I WAS GOING TO ASK FOR A RAISE. A BIG ONE.

SHELLI

Hiroto stormed into my boudoir while I was practicing my "7 exercises for better sex" with Señor Velasquez.

"I want a raise!" he said in an uncharacteristically loud voice. Normally he was so refined and elegant I could hardly hear him, but now I had to cover my ears.

"Hiroto, this is quite unlike you, making me do something. You know how I dislike that. I'm quite hurt."

He then said something so quietly I didn't know what he said so I assumed it was an apology.

"Call *Levin, Levine and Lavine* and tell them what you want..."

HIROTO

SHE GASPED IN THAT VACUUM CLEANER WAY OF HERS WHEN SHE'S CLIMAXING, THEN LAY PANTING AS I LEFT HER WITH AN EXHAUSTED SEÑOR VELASQUEZ.

YASMIN

Yes!

LAWRENCE

I was going to be a father.

Yasmin found the boyfriend ring I made for David and took it to be a surprise engagement ring. I was too surprised about the baby to argue.

Yasmin rarely left my side, which felt like old times when we were just besties except maybe a little more suffocating.

I liked the idea of having children, and when we were younger and thought I was only gay, we'd talked about her having a baby for my husband and me. So this wasn't so different except now I was going to be her husband.

My mother cried when I told her.

"I'm glad you're happy mama."

"I'm not happy you little nitwit, I'm sad you're going to go through life pretending to be straight like your..." she didn't finish the sentence.

"Like my what, mama?"

"Nothing, forget I said it. Blessings to you both." She hung up quickly.

"Your mother must be thrilled, I know mine is!"

"She cried," I said, confused.

"Tears of joy, like me!" Yasmin threw her arms around me and kissed my face 29 times. I know, I counted, wondering when she was going to stop.

"Are you sure about this?" I asked her.

"Sure about what? The baby? Yes. Our love? Yes. Why, aren't you?"

"Um... yyyeeesss," I said, trying to sound sure. I had always loved Yasmin. Nothing had changed—except everything.

JEZ

I was surprised when Tedd called. We talked—I would bill him my usual hourly rate. Then he said he needed some "physical therapy," which I thought was code for dick. But as soon as I put my 8" cock in his face he started to cry.

I pulled my TrimLine boxer briefs back on and sat in my therapist's chair. "We clearly need another talk session." I started my timer.

TEDD

Jez was a mistake. A terrible mistake. The first time and this time. I don't know what I was thinking.

"I think the reason I was attracted to you the first time is that you were kind of an anti-David," I told Jez while looking down at my limp dick.

"I see," he said. Which is what he usually said. Now that I thought about it, he never said very much that was useful.

"What do you see?" I asked him.

"I see you are unaroused."

"A cat would see I was unaroused, Jez. What do you, as a trained professional, or at least a professional because you charge money, or maybe you're just a whore, what do you see?"

"I see your anger, Tedd."

"Again, a cat could see my anger."

"You are projecting your anger onto me." Jez said, sounding more like someone who had a faint idea what they were talking about, or had at least watched a show on Netflix where a character went to a therapist.

"No, I'm angry about you. With you. I'm angry that you forced me to leave David, you motherfucking worthless piece of shit!"

"That's good, let it all out," he said, completely calm. That's when I jumped over the coffee table and tried to strangle him.

"Is that good?" I asked him, my hands wrapped around his throat. He was turning red and unable to speak. I let go before I did any permanent damage because even at my advanced age I was still too pretty to go to jail.

He coughed. He tried to speak. He coughed some more.

I dressed, put a $20 bill on the coffee table and left.

DAVID

So... Tedd told me he went to see Jez and made a big deal about how he *hadn't* fucked him (this time), like he deserved a medal for keeping it in his pants. For Tedd that *was* an accomplishment, but still.

On one hand, I thought, "Our communication skills are vastly improved now. I am pleased he was able to come clean to me about his feelings and actions." I saw this as a very positive sign.

On the other hand I thought, "Oh, my fucking God, I am the world's stupidest human being to have let him back in my life—I wish he was dead."

I said, "Thank you for sharing that with me," went to the kitchen to make dinner... and sharpened the butcher knife.

"Are we really OK?" he asked me in what I perceived to be sincerity, which only pissed me off. If I was writing this scene, or at least a similar scene with an unfaithful husband, I would have written that exact pathetic line! He seriously thought that his "good behavior" and confession would clear the air and make everything better.

Tedd was a complex character in a very simple way. As long as I remembered it was all about him and how people perceived him, I was fine. He honestly didn't want me to think badly of him, even though he'd acted badly. "Hate the sin, love the sinner," the saying goes, though if *he'd* said that I would have chased him around with a cast iron skillet, not the knife, because I couldn't trust myself with that at the moment.

"I don't actually know at the moment, Tedd. That's the honest truth. I do know I don't feel like making dinner."

"Oh, of course, right, sure, let me take you out to dinner at Chateau Marmont, I'm friends with the maître d' who'll slip us in."

"That's so nice of him. Is it because you slipped it in him?"

"Not recently, no!" he protested. The word "recently" literally made me laugh out loud.

"What's your definition of *recently*, Tedd?"

He put his hand over his mouth, thinking. He often did that, as if to keep himself from saying something stupid before he'd thought it over and come up with a better story.

He removed his hand, "Before Jez." Then realization hit his eyes because he remembered that Jez was *supposed* to be his first indiscretion, and he jabbered, "When I was with him... Jez... and..." his hand went back over his mouth. "I promise, I didn't sleep with Jez *this time!*"

I laughed again, stopped suddenly and growled. "Get out."

He stared at me blankly. "What? Why? I... I'm sorry, I thought..."

"You thought? That's so unusual for you. Was it painful?"

"I'm trying to be good now," he said, again so sincerely it was sad. "I love you and it's just sex. You know that. I always come home to you."

"I'm sorry Teddy." I hadn't called him that since we were teenagers, but he seemed like an immature kid. "You're right, it's just sex." He looked relieved. "But I'm looking for love. I wonder where Lu is..." I stopped.

Tedd had been so overwhelming that I hadn't thought about Lu in a bit and when I did, I deflated like a balloon, sitting on the nearest thing, a glass topped end table, something I ordinarily would never have done.

But now I sat there having a fantasy about starting over and living with Lu. How quiet it felt with him— so unlike Tedd's constant buzz. It could be like having a brand new life, one based on kindness and consideration rather than turning a blind eye to a man I'd once heard tell a friend, "I'm a wild stallion, longing to be free."

I heard something crack first—then I fell through the glass table, shards digging into my ass. I tried to extricate myself from the table but was stuck.

I looked around and Tedd was gone.

HIROTO

I made David lie in the back of the Rolls on the pet pad normally reserved for Poofter. Shelli loved David and all,

BUT SHE STILL WOULDN'T BE HAPPY IF HE BLED ON HER BESPOKE CHAMPAGNE LEATHER SEATS.

SHELLI

I took the liberty of having David admitted into a deluxe suite on Cedars Sinai's exclusive eighth floor, reserved for the very famous or at least very rich. One of the Kardashians was next door, either giving birth or getting Botox, it was hard to tell which from her screams.

I had David put in the Claes Oldenburg suite, filled with the artist's original drawings because I knew he was one of David's favorites. I had the resident Michelin starred chef whip up a little *Coq au Champagne* and chocolate souffle just in case I... or David... was peckish.

"Where's Tedd?" was the first thing my poor, dopey boy asked.

"Why do you care?" I replied, putting a quarter of a petit four into his mouth. I'd had Hiroto cut them up in small pieces so they were easier to swallow.

"I don't."

"Oh, yes you do, you silly thing. Or you wouldn't have asked."

"No, I just wanted to make sure he hadn't taken the silverware. I would have!" he said. He started to giggle and couldn't stop. "Ooh it hurts!"

"If you don't stop you're going to bust your stitches," I told him sternly. That only made him laugh more, which made me laugh, which made Hiroto laugh which made a nurse come in.

"What's all this commotion?" a svelte 5'11" Swedish supermodel Nurse Ratched asked. She was breathtaking, as were all the nurses, female and male, on the eighth. Theirs was the prize position for RNs angling to marry a movie star, rapper, CEO or drug lord who had the clout and money to stay on this floor.

"Don't bother with him" I told her, "He's only a screenwriter." She looked very disappointed. "But at least he's funny," I added, as she sadly wafted out of the room on a cloud of her own loveliness.

"Why don't you call Lu?" I asked him.

"He's with his hunky cowboy. I don't want him to come out of pity."

"We're so different in that way, dear. I'm happy for them to come for any reason."

"You dirty girl," he said, wanly.

"And don't you forget it," I whispered, tucking him in. It was only after I'd made the effort that I remembered Hiroto was in the room and could have done it. But I liked doing it for my boy.

TEDD

I went to see David at Cedars. Only Shell could have arranged to get him on the celebrity floor. I brought him See's candy which he used to love but he hardly ate, so I finished the box then joked I'd have to let out my pants. He laughed.

Nurse Magnusson, a strapping six foot two Nordic God of a man came in and said, "I need to change your bandage now, David."

"Thank you, Leif," David replied.

They were on a first-name basis? Oh, this was bad. I could compete against a half-baked 28 year old, but how could I compete against this fully-cooked Adonis?

"You'll need to leave, sir," he said to me, stressing the word *sir* as if I was an 80 year old man.

I slunk out, thinking, "Adonis won't be too excited, David has a flat ass."

LEIF

I'd written this screenplay...

DAVID

Leif gave me his screenplay, entitled *The Boy from Trollheim*. Normally I'd never accept a screenplay from a stranger. I'd heard stories about writers being sued after the fact by would-be writers who said they stole their idea. But Leif explained it was about his boyhood in Trollheim, Norway, and I knew I'd never write a coming-of-age script set in the tundra, so I said I'd take a look.

I didn't expect much, I mean, Leif was a specimen of physical perfection from his golden hair to his toes—though I hadn't seen his toes, and, coming from a place called Trollheim, they might have been huge and hairy, but it didn't matter. His face was chiseled, his chest was sculpted, and his hands...

A lot of men have foot fetishes, I have a hand fetish. Lu's were slim and elegant, like a classic pianist's. Leif's hands were strong and pale and his fingernails were buffed to a subtle sheen. I wanted to kiss them. I shook when he touched me, causing him to put another blanket on me until I was roasting.

Before I even opened the script to read I was thinking of nice things I could say in case it was terrible. I didn't like to lie. "I'm stunned!" was one of my favorite lines when I'd see a friend's film and knew it was not only terrible but bound to be a bomb. They'd always smile, because "stunned' doesn't mean "bored," which is what they are usually most afraid of.

But what if "stunned" was too big of a word for Leif? What if I discovered his grasp of the English language was tentative at best? "I cried," that's a shorter word that still sounded good— even if it was a comedy.

I opened the cover and began to read about snow. Three full pages about snow. This was not a good sign.

LEIF

I've always had a thing for smart guys.

I mean, if I wanted to look at a specimen of physical perfection I could look in the mirror. I don't mean that in a narcissistic way, I simply mean that I know

most people only see the body that I have worked so
hard on.

But I have also worked hard on my screenplay. I have
read books and taken classes. I have lifted well-known
screenwriters like weights.

But they never read past the third page. I would ask
them a question and they'd have "an important call"
and I'd never hear from them again.

Hollywood was a horrible place and I was fed up. I'd
spent the last week looking online at real estate in
Norway. If I moved far enough north I could buy a
timber lodge on 500 hectares for less than the $24,000
annual rent on my tiny studio apartment overlooking
the 101 freeway in East Hollywood.

DAVID

I almost didn't make it past page 3, but on page 4 Leif's mother
was killed by a reindeer sled, and as horrible as that sounds, he
made it absolutely hilarious— blaming it on Santa Claus.

When reading a script you can never tell for sure if it'll be a good
movie—but this felt like a sure-fire hit to me, combining an orphan
and Santa Claus... it was the perfect clean comedy! Marc would
buy this in a Norway minute! He didn't deserve it, but he was also
well-placed to sell this thing internationally.

LEIF

"I want to executive produce your film," David said to
me. I checked his chart to make sure he wasn't
hallucinating under morphine. Nope.

He said, "To tell you the truth, the first three pages could use some cutting. I understand how the 27 types of Nordic snow are eventually integral to the plot, but I've thought of a fun way to show that in a series of shots— think Amelie with frostbite— and then we're off!"

The room started to spin. I felt faint.

DAVID

Leif fainted *on* me, which I imagine is what it feels like to be pinned down by a Yeti—Surprising, a little hard to breathe, but warm and not entirely unpleasant.

The other nurses came in looking like they'd escaped from a Calvin Kline print ad. It took three of the men to lift Leif off me. I didn't ask why it was necessary for them to take off their shirts to do this.

MARC

David waltzed into my office and announced, "I want 10% of the gross, an executive producer credit, plus script, cast and director approval. Or I walk," He said it like he was somebody.

"The fuck you do!" I told him in no uncertain terms.

"You're gonna be sorry you didn't consider it." the pushy bastard said.

While I was considering, he walked.

J. MICHAEL

Yesterday I got my hands on a purloined copy of a script called *Trollheim*. After several exhaustive hours of searching and replacing character names, as well as translating all of Santa Claus' lines to his native Klingon, I finished my latest script, entitled *Trollville*.

DAVID

Having worked Cedars' eighth floor I was sure Leif must have better connections than I did. He claimed he didn't.

"You must have taken care of somebody important," I grilled Leif. "Somebody who was always on the phone? Somebody who seemed too dull or ugly to have famous movie star visitors but did?"

LEIF

"I remember a man with an unfortunate face who had a lot of pretty boys visiting,' I told David. "He was always hitting on me but I told him I couldn't because it was against hospital rules but it was really because he looked like a troll. I know, I grew up with them. They're nasty."

David said, "Bingo!"

I found his chart. Oscar Kremnitz, head of production at Universal. "I don't want to kiss him," I explained.

David calmed me. "You just need to flirt. It's your script that's going to fuck him."

DAVID

I was excited but also felt bad. I'd had 22 movies made yet I wouldn't have been able to get a meeting with Oscar Kremnitz. One text from Leif and he made time for us the next day!

When I told my agent, Queenie, that I got a meeting with Kremnitz, she said, "Who'd you have to fuck, baby doll?"

"I just had to bust my ass," I said, laughing because I really had busted it, though it started to feel better almost immediately after reading Leif's script.

Leif asked, "What should I wear to our meeting?"

I almost said, "As little as possible," but this man was not just a piece of ass, he was an exceptional writer *and* piece of ass.

"Should I buy a new suit?" he continued, nervously.

"Nope. The only people who dress up are lawyers and even then, the more clout they have the less formally they dress. Wear jeans and a t-shirt. A *tight* t-shirt. And what do your feet look like?" He texted me a picture of his feet. Not surprisingly they were perfect. "Wear sandals."

OSCAR

Who could forget Nurse Leif Magnusson? I have an especially warm memory of him changing my dressings!

Usually I have no problem getting young men, but he insisted it would be unprofessional behavior and he could lose his job. So when he called and asked to "meet" with me, I thought, "Gotcha!"

He arrived, looking delicious in tight jeans and a tight T. He was accompanied by a nebbish, also in jeans and T but I didn't care, I couldn't tear my eyes off of Leif.

"What can I do for you?" I asked in my most majestic tone—one that usually had the effect of melting the clothes right off aspiring actors and the occasional screenwriter. Only occasional because screenwriters tend to be a homely lot so who can be bothered?

"Leif's got a sure fire hit of a script," the nebbish said. I didn't bother to look at him, because I was simply stunned by the sight of Leif breathing. The movement of his chest and stomach... his nipples protruding and his belly button doing the opposite of protruding, I couldn't remember the word.

"And what is he willing to give me to read it?" I asked, always negotiating.

"The chance to produce the biggest moneymaker of the year," or so said the nebbish who was now starting to annoy me.

DAVID

I looked the egotistical troll in the eyes and whispered, "The next time you're on the eighth floor with a value-size Baby Ruth stuck up your ass I imagine you're going to want help from the nursing staff. If so, I suggest you read Leif's script."

OSCAR

Blackmail. I respected that. "I'll give it a thorough read, Leif. Because I like you."

J. MICHAEL

Was utterly shocked and insulted when Oscar at Universal claimed he "Already had a script just like it."

Told my agent we should sue.

DAVID

Oscar sent Leif a text the very next day, "Read it. Love it. Want to buy it. Call me!"

I called my agent, Queenie. "Kremnitz is going to make an offer. Whatever he says, ask for double."

I emailed her assistant the rest of my demands and he printed them out because Queenie was old-school and didn't know from email. The bottom of my list had a note, "If he balks, use the secret word: *Baby Ruth.*"

He did. She did.

She called me an hour later. "I'm not going to ask what that meant, I'm just going to say *Mazel Tov, boychik* and let you know my commission is going to a worthy cause: a little antique Faberge necklace that I've had my eye on. It was owned by a Czarina until she lost her head."

I was going to explain, "They didn't use the guillotine, Queenie, they shot..." But it didn't matter. "Wear it in good health," I told her.

LEIF

I couldn't believe it when David called! Two million dollars, minus Queenie's 10% and David's

20% finder's fee which they earned every penny of. Thankfully, my divorce was finalized last month, or my greedy ex would want a chunk of it. Ha! He should have been nicer to me!

I called my father and told him. There was silence at the end of the line and I was afraid he'd had another heart attack but he was just in shock. I told him I could finally buy him the goat farm he'd always wanted. I could even afford a townhouse in Oslo for myself!

I went over to David's and he explained what came next.

DAVID

I explained to him that I had negotiated contractual rights to approve the script, the casting, and the director so they couldn't fuck it up. As it was his story, I would confer with him on all the above to make sure he was happy with it.

"Why are you so nice?" Leif asked, touching my arm and making me tingle.

"I've been screwed too many times. And not in a good way. I don't want that to happen to a good writer like you."

Leif kissed me so forcefully it knocked me off my chair. He picked me up like I was a child and carried me into the bedroom.

"Leif, we really shouldn't." I said, explaining. "I've seen too many movies fucked up from fucking. I want this movie to be as great as your script, so we're not going there."

He set me down on the bed and sat on the edge. "Thank you, David. But I'm a grown ass man and I want…"

I remembered what Shelli had said to me after I'd claimed to be "a grown ass man," and stopped him right there.

OSCAR

Huh. Leif refused my advances. Nobody does that—it made me want him even more.

ZORN

David has completely forgotten about us Stunning Aliens!

DAVID

In the midst of all this excitement I'd completely forgotten about *Stunning Aliens*.

I reread the 20 pages I'd already written and felt nauseous. They weren't very good. At least not as good as *The Boy from Trollheim*. Maybe I'd been distracted by Cubby and Tedd and… I didn't want to even think of Lu's name, but I couldn't help myself. Lu. Sweet. Damn!

Maybe I'd just forgotten how to write anything good after my years writing clean comedies. Or maybe I'd simply forgotten how to write but could now luckily be a producer of someone else's script. Ooh, that made me sad, even though my *Trollheim* salary and points meant I didn't have to bother putting in a pool. I could buy the house next door that already had one.

I imagined naked pool parties to rival George Cukor's and smiled— then felt a tear roll down my cheek as I once again missed Lu and wondered if I'd ever write again.

I loved writing. It was the place I escaped to when the real world wasn't right. But the real world was looking bright, and my writing was getting dim.

Maybe I was an alien because everyday I found people more and more strange.

NORZ

Nipples are ridiculous on men.

DAVID

We were shooting *Trollheim* in Toronto and it was a relief to get away. I realized I'd always been a good producer because I'd done this same work on my clean comedies only I never got credit. Now I was getting credit and money and control!

When the directors I approached turned their noses up at what they saw as a children's film, Shelli recommended her old friend Tarsem Nova. He'd become famous for his artsy music videos and understood the story was deeper than the surface story about Santa Claus. Plus, his gorgeous, fanciful visual style felt just right for the piece.

I even got my dream cast, Diane Keaton as Mrs. Claus and Robert Pattinson as the adult Leif. It was all coming together and felt like a hit!

TARSEM

I MET SHELLI AND HIROTO WHEN WE WERE IN THE PEACE CORPS TOGETHER IN GHANA BUILDING HOUSES,

THAT'S WHEN SHELLI ENCOURAGED ME TO MAKE MY FIRST MUSIC VIDEO FOR A LOCAL BAND WHO CALLED THEMSELVES "EYE, EYE, EYE," THE LOCAL TERM FOR "HOW ARE YOU?"

SHELLI WAS OLDER, A VOLUPTUOUS AND BEAUTIFUL EARTH MOTHER. WE ALL FELL IN LOVE WITH HER, BUT SHE WAS FOCUSED ON MAKING THE WORLD A BETTER PLACE WITH HER BARE HANDS.

THEN SHE MET MAGNUS, A SWEDISH OIL MAGNATE IN GHANA SCOUTING TO DRILL FOR OIL. HE IMMEDIATELY FELL FOR HER AND SWEPT HER OFF HER FEET TO PARIS WHERE HE WINED, DINED AND WED HER.

NOW SHE COULD MAKE THE WORLD BETTER BY USING HER BARE HANDS TO WRITE HUGE CHECKS TO CHARITIES. SHE WAS A GOOD HUMAN BEING, PURE OF HEART UNDERNEATH ALL THAT WEALTH.

SO WHEN SHE RECOMMENDED ME TO DAVID I KNEW HE MUST BE A GOOD GUY, TOO. WE TALKED FOR HOURS ABOUT OUR VISION FOR TROLLHEIM AND I WAS SO HAPPY BECAUSE I FINALLY HAD A CHANCE TO MAKE A HOLLYWOOD MOVIE, EVEN IF IT WAS SHOT IN TORONTO.

DAVID

I had no idea Toronto was just across a lake from Niagara Falls! Like so many, my parents had their honeymoon at Niagara Falls. Their life went downhill from there, or at least starting with their little "bundle of oy"—me. As a kid I used to think I was responsible for their unhappiness.

DORY

Months ago I told David that his parents' unhappiness wasn't his fault—he was just a kid. He knew I was right but wouldn't let go.

Me, I'd learned to let go. I said I'd be gone for a month and it had been three.

I set up auto replies on my text and email, "I'm sorry, my code of ethics does not allow me to conduct therapy via text, David."

DAVID

After we wrapped for the night I called my mother. I'd been so busy I actually forgot I had one. This was aided by the fact that I set my phone to automatically send all her calls to voicemail.

"Oh, so you're still alive," she whined. It wasn't so much a whine as a kind of piercing screech. The tone of her voice always made me need to pee really badly.

I'd asked Dory about that once and *thought* she said something about "salmon" and I felt too dumb to ask her to explain.

DORY

I'd either said, "maman" because I was thinking of my own mother, or "mamón" which is what she called me in Spanish, which translated to "idiot." I was not going to be a mamón now and answer David's calls now.

DAVID

I googled "salmon" later, and thought she was trying to explain how adaptable a salmon's kidneys are— they work harder and pee a lot when they're in freshwater streams. But in the ocean, and I quote, "Their urine production rates drop dramatically and the urine is as concentrated as the kidneys can make it." Dory is very wise. I wish she'd return my calls.

Mother said that she wished that Dad was dead, as if that was news. This was the first time I wondered why she was "Mother" and he was "Dad." I hadn't heard from Dad since I came out at 16 and according to Doris Applebaum, our old next door neighbor and later, I found out, his mistress, he'd moved to Argentina to hunt Nazis. I always wondered if he'd found any, but when I googled his name I only got a cardiologist in Queens who claimed licorice was a miracle cure for gout.

I'd always liked licorice and never had gout. Related?

Mother talked for 25 minutes without taking a breath. At least that's how it sounded. As she talked I looked at available men on Scruff. If they were at all interesting I clicked on the little paw button which was shorthand for "*Woof*," which was gay bear shorthand for "Hi, Handsome!" In my experience you had to *Woof* at 50 men before one Woofed back.

That was OK, to me it was like online shopping. "Oh, look at this cute ginger bear in a speedo. He likes growing lettuce and BDSM. Seems sweet." Or "Palestinian looking for Israeli to take it up the ass for world peace." Some of these were very specific.

And then I saw him. *Lu*. Smiling. Only 12 miles away. His relationship status said, "engaged." It was only a matter of time. The first time a cute cowboy appeared I would have lost him anyway. I was an idiot and didn't deserve him. It's just as well I saved myself the heartbreak by breaking my own heart first.

LAWRENCE

I'd always liked Yasmin's parents. They were nice— they ran a chain of dry cleaners in Toronto called "Out Out Damn Spot!" Their mascot was Shakespeare but instead of holding a pen, he held a tube of "environment friendly" spot remover.

Her father, Azad, had a speedboat and liked to carve portraits of famous dead people in his spare time, his most recent being of *Rumi*. He was proud of how much it looked like the actual man but there was no way to tell since Rumi died hundreds of years ago and there were no realistic paintings made during his lifetime. Besides, all Azad's carved portraits tended to look the same. It didn't matter—he loved making them. There was a lesson in that somewhere. I wished Dory would come back from that retreat.

Azad gave me a scroll with one of Rumi's poems on it:

> *O soul, If thou, too, wouldst be free,*
> *Then love the Love that shuts thee in.*
> *'Tis Love that twisteth every snare;*
> *'Tis Love that snaps the bond of sin;*

I would make the barbed wire piece I drew in Wyoming, inscribe this poem on it and give it to Yasmin. Then again, when I showed her the drawing once and she said, "Ick," so I didn't think she'd wear it, but then I would. It would make a good *memento vitae* and remind me how every day of life with Yasmin was making me free!

Azad offered me a job managing his East York dry cleaner location. That was very kind of him, but I explained that I was going to be a geologist and jewelry designer and he said, "Fine. Go do that, then."

Yasmin said I'd hurt his feelings so I apologized and accepted the job. I could design jewelry when I retired. Yamin's mother was elated, saying they would buy the house next door for us. Love did twisteth the snares.

DAVID

I couldn't help it. I had to click on his profile picture. I swiped down his other pics: Lu looking cute at the beach. Lu looking cute with a tiny pick in his hand when he went digging for diamonds in Arkansas. Lu looking cute in his blue velvet suit... wait, that was from when we went to see the musical version of *The Shawshank Redemption* on Broadway. It closed after one performance. I recognized my elbow—he cut me out of the picture!

I was all ready to click on the little paw button to send him a *Woof* when his pictures were suddenly replaced with a notice, "Profile deleted."

I sobbed in my trailer, stopping only to wonder if it was making the trailer shake so much that it might look like I was fucking someone. That sounded better than sobbing. And was there a better way of forgetting about Lu? I couldn't think of one at the moment.

So I stopped at craft services, got a prune Danish and took it to Harry, the bearded hipster grip who went out of his way to bring me a prune Danish every morning, unasked. Also, either he was hitting on me or just being nice, so me handing him a Danish was either flirting or just nice.

Turned out that Harry wanted more than the Danish in his mouth. We started with my tongue and moved on from there.

Later, there was a knock on the door of my trailer and Kelly, the first AD, loudly whispered, "Harry, we need you on set," so clearly it was no secret. Ah, well...

HARRY

David was exactly my type—a brainy bear. He was smart, creative and I liked the gray in his beard.

He was a good producer. Solved personality and production problems and never yelled at anybody. I crushed on him fast, thinking about how we could have a "Harry and David" blog.

I'd been screwing around with immature guys and other crew members for so long that the idea of a real *man* lit my fire. I wanted to settle down and be a house husband: cook, clean, do laundry, remodel, workout in our home gym and take care of my man. Adopt kids or share them with our lesbian couple friends.

I tended to jump right into relationships—thinking they'd be like my fantasies. So far they *never* were, but maybe this time... I'd be lucky, maybe this time he'd stay! I found myself humming that Liza Minelli song all day, except during takes when Ray, the sound man would have killed

me.

YASMIN

Life was going to be perfect— I was having twins!

DAVID

I hadn't gotten over Lu, the way he made me feel and the way I felt about him—Love.

I didn't love Harry, but I liked having him around. Maybe that was enough. So maybe the key to my life wasn't learning how to be happily in love and still write, but to stop with the love and writing and just learn to be happy!

HARRY

I suggested David make me his personal assistant and he did. Wow. How cool to carry around an iPad instead of schlepping heavy lights. How easy to bring David organic snacks so he wouldn't fill up on chips and candy bars. It was trippy watching David do his thing.

DAVID

The director, Tarsem, was a small man (only 5' tall) with a large presence. He was a lovely, gentle visionary, but he needed a lot of hand-holding.

Robert and Diane were playing house, which was dangerous in case they had a falling out, but I made sure they didn't.

I sent Diane a vintage Eames chair for her trailer and made it look like it was from Robert. Meanwhile, Robert didn't know that the library of vintage vinyl jazz albums Diane supposedly sent actually came from me, too. On-set they pretended just to be colleagues but everybody knew what was going on between them.

HARRY

Everyone knew what was going on with David and me. Or I made sure they did.

I also made sure he got enough sleep (he always slept well after fucking), and had a good organic, locally sourced artisanal breakfast (not the Costco pastries from the crafty table).

David called me his major domo: I managed his appointments, dry cleaning, and most importantly, made sure that he took breaks/naps.

I thought he must be falling in love with me and we were going to go back to LA and live happily ever after.

LAWRENCE

Traditionally, the groom was not supposed to see the wedding dress before the wedding, but Yasmin kept texting me pictures of her mother's choices and I knew if I didn't step in she was going to look like something on the top of a wedding cake—fluffy.

I knew what Yasmin wanted. Sleek and sexy without being slutty because we both agreed there was nothing worse than a slutty bride unless it was a groom in shorts. Ugh. So after her mother bought her a Lady Di meets Barbie wedding dress, Yasmin and I went on a secret shopping mission and bought her a modest but form-fitting nude lace, high-neck, ankle length with a side slit dress. It featured long but transparent sleeves so you could see what great arms she had, like Jennifer Garner and Michelle Obama. In fact, she took me to the gym and taught me how to add definition to my guns.

It was all planned that on the day of the wedding she would spill a glass of wine down the front of the poofy dress and as luck would have it, Esme, one of her bridesmaids, would have this backup dress handy.

I loved Yasmin as a friend, but wasn't sure I could be the best husband to her because I wasn't *in love* with her. I hadn't gotten over David.

But Yasmin's father had told me that the most important secret to being the perfect husband was simply to say "yes dear," to whatever your wife said, for the rest of your life. I could do that.

ZORN

David's writing was too sporadic and slow. I considered jumping into J. Michael's brain, but was concerned he would simply search and replace my name into another script and I'd end up speaking Klingon, which wasn't even what the real Klingons I knew spoke. J. Michael would be done faster but I needed to get *my* message across.

Because David stopped listening to me, my only option was to appear in his dreams.

Each night I'd tell him more of my story. How Norz and I started out as Instagram influencers and quickly amassed over a million followers. But the more perfect our pictures appeared, the more backlash there was against us not being *authentic*, or flaunting our *privilege.*

We had great engagement numbers, but the comments became so caustic it actually caused a piece of my face to melt. It was relatively easy to repair using the blood of a virgin, but disturbing nonetheless.

DAVID

Maybe it was stress, but I was having weird dreams. I wrote them down because Dory recommended I do this. As our month-anniversary present, Harry was able to track her down in Nova Scotia where she'd become a Buddhist nun.

Harry arranged for a private jet to take us to her monastery and when we showed up the look on her face was priceless. She was in the middle of a silent meditation and couldn't talk to us, but we waited. Turned out they made an amazing cider there which Harry wanted to package and promote as *Nun Better Cider!*, exclamation mark and all.

Harry didn't realize the entire monastery was silent all the time. So even when Dory came to see us she couldn't talk. I wrote on Harry's iPad and showed it to Dory who shook her head, "no," then wrote her reply, "I can no longer be your therapist, David, but if you want to do something useful, the monastery needs a new walk-in freezer. "

I wrote, "I understand you can't talk, but if I buy you a new freezer would you be able to ~~provide therapy~~, *advise* me via text?"

She looked at the floor then nodded slowly. Harry arranged for a new freezer the very next day and Dory, who now called herself Pema Sita, started replying to my texts.

DORY (AKA PEMA SITA)

Oy.

DIANE KEATON

I knew David sent me the chair, I didn't care. It was an original
Eames Lounge chair which differs from the later models in the use
of pure Amazonian rubber spacers as opposed to the later plastic.
I loved the chair.

I didn't love Robert but he could be fun. He got very silly when he
was drunk, which was basically every night. We like to play
Twister.

ROBERT PATTINSON

Diane was a gas. She gave me a cool collection of vinyl. I liked to
drink till I couldn't see straight and listen to Dizzy Gillespie. Most
nights involved a spirited game of naked Twister, which was handy
because the twister board thing or whatever you call it was plastic
and by around 2am I tended to puke on it.

HARRY

Twister was my idea. Easy cleanup.

LEIF

I watched some footage and loved what Tarsem was doing with the film, he really understood the vision of my script.

But I found the filming beyond tedious, especially when I was under pressure to choose tile and fixtures for my new Oslo townhouse.

Diane was very sweet, though she asked me if she could change a few lines. I asked why. She said, "Because I'm not a good enough actress to say it the way you wrote it." I said, "sure," and she gave me a hand-knit cap and a scarf she made. Robert looked puffy.

ZORN

For 16 nights in a row I gave David the same dream: Santa was an alien. How else could he fly around the world and deliver all those presents in one night— he had the power to bend time and space. The dream would end with a closeup on Santa's face, which was mine with a long white beard.

DAVID

The pressure was getting to me. I was having an uncomfortable dream over and over. About Santa.

Tarsem made a spectacular film. I worked with the editor to tighten it up in post. The effects for the scene where Santa and Leif fly through the northern lights made me cry, partially because the first VFX house went belly up and I had to find another ASAP, but also because WetaFX jumped into the fray and did such a stunning job.

Stunning. Aliens. Oh. Now I remember the dream. Now I remember my script. I was unhappy. I had to write.

DORY AKA PEMA SITA

I texted David: Unhappiness is not a prerequisite for creative energy, David.

David: Yes, but it's when I write best.

Me: How do you know?

David: Because I write more when I'm miserable.

Me: More, or better?

I watched the dot dot dot of WhatsApp.

David: I don't know.

Me: Good.

David: I guess I could try writing while happy.

Me: Do not try—do.

I know, the last text was a little Yoda, but he could be wise despite sounding like Miss Piggy.

DAVID

Harry moved into my rented townhouse in Toronto. He took care of me while also starting his *Nun Better Cider!* company.

He wasn't Lu but I was happy *enough*. I tried writing.

INT. ZORN AND NORZ'S LOFT - NIGHT

The white loft now appears dark blue, lit only by
the night sky and lights of LA. Zorn stands at
the window, looking in horror at his phone as
nasty comments fly by. "What are you? CGI?" "You
probably aren't even human!" "Go back where you
came from!" "Where'd you get those rad
sunglasses?" "I'm only 6 and I already hate you!"

The last comment takes him aback, and he drops
the phone in shock. It falls 22 stories down and
smashes through the roof of a shiny new Rolls
Royce. A rapper jumps out, rubbing his head, and
looks at the damage to his ride.

                    RAPPER
          I coulda been kilt. Glory
          be to God!

He gets back in the car, looks up through the
hole in the roof then burns rubber and jets away.

Zorn's face lights up—literally glowing, dare I
say, a heavenly light.

                    ZORN
          Gods!

CUT TO: INSERT SHOT OF ZORN'S INSTAGRAM PAGE

All the old posts disappear. In their place are
posts featuring faces of real people of all ages,
ethnicities and genders, glowing blissfully above
the repeated meme, "BETTER ANGELS, BETTER LIFE!"

FAST MOTION: As more posts are added, the
followers counter ticks ever higher. As it ticks
higher, B-list celebrity faces start to appear in
the posts, their ecstatic faces seeming to
emanate light.

The follower count passes 200 million. A-list celebrities are enraptured.

ZOOM IN ON a single post of Zorn with his hands reaching up to the heavens.

DISSOLVE INTO VIDEO OF THE POST

             ZORN
       My fellow angels!

ZOOM BACK TO SHOW STADIUM-SIZED MEGACHURCH, EVERY SEAT FILLED.

Pan across the celebrity studded front row, with a Kardashian-like clan with tight dresses and tight faces filling half the row.

             ZORN
       Future
       generations will
       look back on
       this time as
       golden! A time
       when we were
       changing the
       world for the
       better. A time
       when we became
       the global
       revolution to
       spread love and
       make it both
       spiritual and
       physical!

The crowd cheers.

             ZORN
       Let us all sing together the
       watchword of our people.

Everyone begins to sing the Beatles' "All you need is love" (all together now!) With each trumpet "da da da da da" Zorn points at audience members. Golden light streams from his fingertips, illuminating a couple in the crowd. Their clothes fall off and they are attracted as if magnetic. They copulate, their hip thrusts knocking into the couple next to them.

FAST MOTION

Like dominoes, one couple couples, then the next, then the next and next and next until they're all falling down, creating a stadium full of sex, a writhing naked orgy.

YASMIN

I was having second thoughts. When my hairdresser, Rashid, touched my head, I felt something I never felt with Boo — serious hotness, I mean like burning hotness, I mean like I'm on-fire inflamed hotness. Being a hunky hairdresser with a glorious mane of hair, I assumed Rashid was gay but then he told me how he just broke up with his girlfriend and I got chills, actual chills. First burning, then chillin'. I thought I might be coming down with something but then he went down on me.

I couldn't remember if Boo and I had agreed on an open relationship. But it didn't matter, because this was only oral, so it didn't count.

LAWRENCE

Despite my agreeing with everything she said, Yasmin was still very crabby. Her mother said it was normal during pregnancy which meant there were only six months more of her unpleasantness. Hopefully six months would be enough time to forget David, because I still had sweet dreams about him.

Thankfully, I was distracted by the dry cleaning job, which was one long series of problems. Luckily the staff I was managing were very nice. There were Indians and Pakistanis working side-by-side. Inspiring. My office didn't have a window so I wouldn't be distracted by looking outside. My job basically consisted of talking to angry people about lost buttons or stains or broken zippers. Lots of broken zippers, which I started to think might have been broken before we did the cleaning.

But our motto was "Our Audience is always right," so my job was to look down, smile, and say, "I'm so, so, sorry, I will take care of it personally." Then I took the offensive garment to Priti or Awani, depending whether it was a spot or zipper, and I was fixed.

That left me a lot of time to draw jewelry, which was good because otherwise I felt tired from being obsequious, not to mention bored out of my mind. The zippers reminded me of the famous *Van Cleef and Arpels* diamond zipper necklace. I had an idea for how to update it for my uncle Fareed's company when I heard yelling from the front of the store and had to apologize to a woman whose dress had shrunk... even though it appeared that she had grown.

I was cheered up when I got home and saw Yasmin looking happy for a change. I complimented her hair, which looked especially voluminous and she said, "I need to have it done more often— it's called *self-care. You* should try it." I would, except I was too busy working for her father.

DAVID

Text to Pema: You were right. I'm relatively happy and still writing better than I ever had before.

DORY AKA PEMA SITA

Text to David: Wonderful! I don't like to say "I told you so" but I did :)

That wasn't the most professional message but I wasn't texting him in a professional capacity anymore and it needed to be said.

Text to David: We need a new heating system.

DAVID

Text to Pema: Thanks. I'll send Harry right over.

OSCAR

The rough cut was shit. Way way way way way way way way way way way way way way way way too long. The poster was awful. Robert looked puffy. I hated the score.

I got David on the horn and verbally blew his brains out.

God, I loved my job!

ZORN

It was good to feel my energy flow through David onto the page. But if he didn't calm the fuck down he was going to have a coronary before he finished the script.

HARRY

The producer and director were both unhappy with the cut. Diane kept calling David because Robert wouldn't stop calling her. I saw the poster and it was terrible, Robert looked puffy.

Nun Better Cider! had a magical effect on me and I couldn't wait to learn more from the monks. I was making daily visits to the monastery and enjoyed the calm after craziness at the studio. David was angry a lot. He didn't get home until 3am and by that time I was sleeping because the nuns and monks woke at dawn.

I read David's script. It was dumb. And he farted in his sleep.

DAVID

Oscar was the devil and I'd sold my soul to him. Now he wanted his due and I felt like I had a rock on my chest.

The poster was shit—Santa looked terrifying, Robert looking alcoholic. Fired the agency. Fired composer Hans Zimmer, he'd never been my choice anyway and his heavy score made the tender moments ominous. Called in my old composer friend Jack Arnold and begged him to make it right.

Was sorry to have fire the editor—it wasn't her fault Oscar was unhappy with the cut. I was working with Tarsem on a new cut but if he had his way the movie would be six hours long.

Robert was texting Diane drunken messages in the middle of the night, at least that's what Diane texted me in the middle of the night, along with cute animal videos and pictures of her newest hats.

I arranged for Robert to go to rehab. He agreed, as long as it included daily massages, gluten-free vegan cappuccinos and special rehab sessions on horseback. So. *Promises* in Malibu it was. Again.

Again. I told them not to let him use his phone. Got Prem Akkaraju at Weta on the phone. He said they had CGI that could make Robert look less puffy but it would cost a million dollars. Oscar said we'd take it out of Robert's salary then make him sue us. Ugh.

I was exhausted and terrified and the Alien screenplay only dribbled out. I had a foreboding feeling.

LAWRENCE

The barbed wire necklace arrived from the goldsmith. It was elegantly rustic, the distressed finish oxidized to give it an aged look. I wanted to show it to Yasmin but it seemed like she was always getting her hair done. I texted a photo to uncle Fareed who replied, "Pretty, but painful?"

I put it on myself and looked in the mirror. *'Tis Love that twisteth every snare.*

It was beautiful. I felt like I was being strangled.

HARRY

Nun Better Cider! had production problems. My contact at the monastery was a young monk named Rhu. He had the most beatific smile. He didn't talk, of course, but his handwriting, like his scent, flowed like the rain pouring down from the heavens.

The next time I saw Rhu I gave him a prune Danish. Our eyes met and it was a cosmic connection.

DAVID

Text to Pema: I am exhausted and angry and unhappy— and not writing.

I thought maybe I should have formed that into some kind of question.

The writing had dried up because I felt uneasy each time I thought about it.

Text to Pema: Zorn appeared in a dream, stabbing me in the heart with a fountain pen. Do you think this means something?

DORY AKA PEMA SITA

I only replied to David's texts at night, after our final prayers. I lay in my narrow bed, darkness all around, and forced myself to turn on the phone, its screen blinding me.

Text to David: Ask yourself what you are afraid of. ~~I am afraid of losing myself replying to your stupid texts late at night.~~

The monastery needed to find another patron because all I wanted was to see the stars.

SHELLI

David didn't sound good on the phone so I asked Hiroto to "fire up the jet." I liked saying that. Hiroto got right out of my bed and arranged it. He was a darling. I asked him to marry me.

HIROTO

Shelli asked me to marry her. I do love her, but I said, "Since your husbands tend to die tragically, I'm going to have to lovingly pass."

She kissed me and gave me a Patek Philippe Grandmaster Sonnerie, a huge, heavy watch that chimed the time. I thought it cost $250,000 but later Googled it and it was $2.2 million.

I told her I wanted to retire but still live with her. Then I called to "fire up the jet." I loved saying that.

DAVID

Shelli arrived in a whirlwind of *Joy* perfume by Jean Patou plus a hint of jet fuel, Hiroto by her side. She pulled my face to her soft breasts which were itchy in her Chanel tweed suit.

"You poor baby," she said, cradling me back and forth.

I purred, like a kitten. "Thank you, Shell, I needed this," I told her, or tried, as she was pressing my face so tightly into her chest it was hard to talk.

"I'm here, my little petit four," she cooed.

She finally released me, which was good because I was feeling light headed from a lack of oxygen.

"I'm under a lot of pressure but I'm fine, really."

She raised her eyebrows. "Bullshit, baby. Where's your little stress relief ball Harry? I'm dying to meet him."

HARRY

Rhu silently showed me how the monks crush the apples with their feet. Feeling them squish between my toes turned me on but Rhu would not allow me to touch him. It was a spiritual experience.

RHU

...

SHELLI

I was worried about my dear Davey Cakes. He was looking frazzled. I flew my facialist, Juanita, in from Madrid. She gave him a once-over and he still looked bad. Worried.

Sent Hiroto to the monastery to find that little shit Harry. Found him in a vat of apples. This is why I only drink fermented juice—alcohol kills the germs.

Spilled red wine on my white Chanel. Asked Hiroto to take it to the Goodwill but now that he's not officially working for me he was firm and said it was wasteful, sent it to a dry cleaner and lectured me for altogether too long about how we had to be cognizant of the environment.

I wrote a check for $12 million dollars to Greenpeace and smacked Hiroto across the face with it. "Feel better now?" I asked him.

HIROTO

I FELT BETTER. I WAS A GOOD INFLUENCE ON SHELLI. TOGETHER WE WOULD WORK TO GIVE ALL HER MONEY AWAY. I WAS NOT GREEDY, I COULD LIVE OFF THE $2.2M WATCH IF I SOLD IT. THIS WAS FUN.

OSCAR

Text to David: If *Trollheim* tanks it's all on you, putz. You won't even be able to get a job at Starbucks, so buckle down and get it done, fucktard.

I'd just discovered the word "fucktard" from my nephew who I got into Stanford. I'd complained to him that there were no truly offensive words anymore.

He texted, "What about *cunt*?"

I texted, "That's what I call my colleagues in London, it's a compliment."

He texted, "FUCKTARD" in all caps. "That's the most offensive thing we can say around here— 100% non-PC."

I texted, "FUCKING PERFECT DUDE," and sent the fucktard a bag of coke for his birthday.

DAVID

Shell kept sending over people to exfoliate me, or worse, flog me with roses (no thorns, but still).

Tarsem's most recent cut came in at eight hours and 27 minutes, yes, two and a half hours *longer*.

I couldn't drink Starbucks anymore.

Harry breezed in, the first time I'd seen him awake in I don't know how long and gave me some cider. I nearly choked on it. It tasted like feet.

HARRY

I told David I was going on a silent retreat for a month.

DAVID

That's what Dory said.

HARRY

Rhu showed me the light. Every night. Without words. Without touch. It was transcendent. We spoke with the silent language of the heart. It helped that the monastery also grew Psilocybin mushrooms. I saw a new business opportunity while feeling at one with the universe.

ZORN

I had to get David writing again! I gave him a dream about Harry and Rhu in the cider.

DAVID

It was a relief to sleep alone in Shell's penthouse suite. I didn't have to worry if Harry had come home or not. He didn't come out and tell me but I had a dream about him and some rando monk. Not sure where the dream came from but—got it.

It would have been nice if he'd told me himself, but he did send a package of magic mushrooms I shared with Shell and Tarsem. Hiroto said he'd watch over us in case anyone decided to jump off the balcony.

Hiroto was a mensch. He said we should set intentions. Tarsem, who looked especially small tonight sitting next to Shelli, said his was to see the universe as it was meant to be. I found that a bit vague. Shell said she wanted to have a fucking great time. Nice and specific.

I said I wanted direction. That's all. And maybe a fucking sign.

We had a lovely cheese tray while we were waiting for the mushrooms to kick in. I particularly enjoyed the creamy Manchego with sweet pink quince paste.

I thought maybe I'd made a mistake and the mushrooms were meant for risotto, but then the fireplace started to talk to me and I thought maybe this was working after all.

The fireplace sounded like Kathleen Turner— smoky. Unfortunately it seemed to be speaking Spanish so I only understood a word here or there. No, wait, it was Portuguese which I didn't understand at all. Then it started singing, still in Portuguese, but I recognized the melody of "The Sound of Music."

Shelli was filled with sparkling blue gems. Or was that her necklace? No, they were inside her. It was pretty. Tarsem was made of glittering rubies while Hiroto was effervescent with diamonds.

I laid down on the floor and closed my eyes. I could see my precious gemstone friends all around me. Even with my eyes closed. I could see the entire room as a 3D model. At the axis of each vertical and horizontal line was the silhouette of a barnyard animal: a cow, a duck, a pig, a chicken, an elephant, a pterodactyl.

I was floating. The music tasted like popcorn.

I felt like I was being held by the universe. I heard a voice say, "when you're being held, you don't have to hold yourself together." I cried opal tears.

SHELLI

This was pretty good stuff, though I'd had better in Tibet with the Dalai Lama.

My dead husbands appeared in paisley suits. They floated in from through the patio doors.

It didn't surprise me that they were flying, just that they were holding hands. Very sweet. I felt tears running down my face and I hoped Hiroto wouldn't be cross with me as they tasted like Chateau Lafite Rothschild '55, a very good year.

Hiroto held me, rocking me back and forth like a baby. I was a baby. Newborn. I had no words for anything yet I knew everything.

HIROTO

SHELLI ASKED IF I WAS ANGRY ABOUT HER TEARS. I TOLD HER OF COURSE NOT. I LOVED HER.

TARSEM HAD TAKEN OFF HIS CLOTHES AND WAS IN THE CORNER, STANDING ON HIS HEAD.

DAVID WAS GETTING PRECARIOUSLY CLOSE TO THE BALCONY SO I PULLED HIM BACK AND TOLD HIM TO LIE ON THE SOFA. HE SAID, "YES, DAD, THANKS, DAD, LOVE YOU, DAD," LICKED MY BIG TOE AND SAID, "YUM."

SHELLI ASKED IF I COULD SEE HER DEAD HUSBANDS. I COULDN'T.

SHE TOLD ME THEY TOLD HER THAT SHE WASN'T CURSED.

TARSEM WAS GONE.

TARSEM

I WAS FLYING!

DAVID

I thought I heard a whooshing noise outside. Or maybe it was Hiroto's refreshing toes. I wanted to take a sip. He pulled them away, which made me think I was meant to suffer. *Life is suffering* is something I remember someone saying sometime. Someone important? Famous, at least. Jim Carrey? Cary Grant? "Carry me down to the water, oh Lord oh Lord," I sang loudly. I'd always loved spirituals as long as they didn't dwell on Jesus' purifying blood which creeped me out.

"Old man river, that old man river," I belted at the top of my voice.

Life is suffering, yes. Proof I was alive! I'd been right all along in knowing I needed to be unhappy to write.

HIROTO

"Tarsem? Tarsem?" He didn't answer. I checked every room, he wasn't there.

I forced myself to look over the edge of the balcony just in case I'd missed him, but I didn't see a mess.

Where was he?

DAVID

Shelli was dancing a waltz all by herself, yelling, "Come dance with me, baby!"

I wasn't sure who she was talking about, so I got up and danced with her. She was quite light on her feet, so light that she was floating in mid-air. I held onto her belt like the string on a balloon. It was getting dark outside but she was still illuminated from within.

LAWRENCE

Azad told me I should always be the last one to leave. I was on my way out when I saw a garment hanging on the "deliver today" rack. Why had it not been delivered? Where was it supposed to go? The Four Seasons Toronto, penthouse. Not too far out of my way home, I'd drop it by myself.

HIROTO

I asked hotel security to look for Tarsem but they came back empty-handed. I told Shell I was worried and she said, "If anything happens to him you can blame it on that fucking hipster, Harry," then she continued to waltz with a sofa

CUSHION AS DAVID WAS SHUFFLING AROUND THE SUITE LICKING THE
DOOR KNOBS.

DAVID

I'd never seen dicks growing out of doors before!

LAWRENCE

I got in the Four Seasons elevator and pressed the penthouse button but it didn't light up. I pressed it harder and it still didn't light up.

I explained to the concierge that the elevator wasn't working and he said it was working as designed because a key was required for penthouse access "to keep out people like you."

I found this very rude. The situation didn't improve when he grabbed the garment from me and said that he would deliver it himself upstairs and that I was free to go.

When I was getting in my car I thought I heard a man singing *Old Man River*.

DAVID

Shell was so graceful. I sang. She danced. I looked over the edge of the balcony. Did I see someone familiar getting into a car? Hiroto pulled me back.

Maybe what I saw was a man being eaten by a car? Or did I want to eat a car? I wanted to lick another doorknob. Ah, that's what those things on the door really were.

"I think I'm coming down," I said to him. He looked relieved. He was so nice. I squeezed his ass and said, "I love you, Hiro."

He squeezed my ass back and said, "Love you, too, Mr. David."

I loved everybody!

OSCAR

I hated everybody.

SHELLI

I felt gravity returning and it made me sad. I found gravity so tiresome. I dropped onto the sofa.

"Oh, my little Davey baby, you're still here!" I said, watching him squeeze Hiroto's ass for an impressively long time.

"I had a lovely time, boys."

Hiroto pried David's hand off his ass and sat down beside me. "I'm glad, love," he said in his sonorous voice that always made me relaxed.

Davey sat on the other side of me and we pressed against each other.

"That was a lovely trip. I'm happy my two favorite men were here with me. I'm sorry it's ending so soon."

DAVID

"We can do it again next week!" I chimed in. "And week after week after week after week!"

I felt an idea expanding inside me, like a balloon or a fire hydrant or a manhole cover exploding.

"Aha!" I said, my brain lighting up with possibilities!

I threw up on the sofa. And carpet. And Shelli. Little pieces of quince paste everywhere, looking like confetti.

HIROTO

I SURE AS HELL WASN'T GOING TO CLEAN THAT UP. I UNDRESSED
SHELL AND PUT HER IN THE PRIMARY BATHROOM TUB. I CALLED
HOUSEKEEPING AND GREETED THE TWO WOMEN AND A MAN AT THE
DOOR WITH FIVE CRISP $100 BILLS EACH. THEN THEY DIDN'T SEEM TO
MIND THE MESS.

DAVID

I dropped my clothes and wanted a bath. Shell was in it but it was
big enough for both of us, so I sank into the suds.

Hiroto joined us.

"Right before I threw up I had a brilliant idea, but I can't
remember what it was," I told them.

Hiroto reminded me, "You were talking about doing this every
week, but now I wonder if that's such a great idea."

I was suddenly sober, though I'd stopped breathing.

"Breathe!" Hiroto said, slapping me on the back, causing me to
swallow some bubbles and choke.

"What're we going to take next week?" Shell asked and I put my
finger to her mouth.

"Let me get this out before I forget it again! Tarsem's version of
Trollheim is over eight hours long. It's beautiful but I see no way
to cut it down to two. It's never going to be a movie!" I announced,
happily.

"Why are you happy about it?" Hiroto asked as if I was still high.

"Because it's a *series!!!*"

HIROTO

Ah!

SHELLI

Burp.

HIROTO

"Speaking of Tarsem, have either of you seen him?"

Neither of them answered as they were making bubble beards on each other's faces.

I got out of the tub and put on a fluffy robe. Not the hotel ones, those weren't as nice as the baby alpaca ones I'd packed. But I'd only brought two, so David would have to suffer.

Housekeeping had already left and there was no trace of David's explosion.

There was a flashing light on the telephone. Maybe it was from Tarsem. No, it was the concierge saying some dry cleaning had arrived and to let him know when to bring it up. I called him and asked if he'd seen a small Indian man go through the lobby and he said, "At least a dozen."

"A naked one," I added.

"Only three," he joked. "I'll have security check the cameras and get back to you."

SHELL AND DAVID WERE SINGING "YO HO, YO HO, A PIRATE'S LIFE FOR ME!" NEXT TIME I WANTED TO JOIN THEM FOR THE TRIP.

THE CONCIERGE ARRIVED. "I HOPE EVERYTHING IS TO YOUR SATISFACTION," HE SAID, SNIFFING AS IF HE SMELLED SOMETHING. HE HANDED ME SHELL'S CHANEL SUIT AND TWO PLASTIC-COATED WIRE RACKS. "THE CLEANER DELIVERED THIS, AND WE FOUND THESE DISHWASHER RACKS IN THE SWIMMING POOL AND SURMISED THEY SOMEHOW FELL OFF YOUR BALCONY."

"YES, THANK YOU... MR. REYNOLDS," I SAID, READING HIS NAME TAG.

"IF YOU DON'T MIND, I'LL PUT THESE BACK IN THE DISHWASHER." REYNOLDS SAID, WITH A BIT OF A SNEER.

HE OPENED THE DISHWASHER AND GASPED. "I BELIEVE YOU ALSO LOST THIS, YES?" REYNOLDS SAID, OPENING THE DOOR TO REVEAL TARSEM, NAKED, EATING A WHEEL OF BRIE AND A DISHWASHING POD.

LATER, WHEN EVERYONE WAS TUCKED SAFELY IN BED I WENT TO HANG UP SHELL'S CHANEL SUIT AND NOTICED A SPOT ON IT.

AZAD

"Hello, this is Azad, owner of *Out Out Damned Spot*. I hear you had an issue with a Chanel suit and wanted to personally apologize and let you know that we will make it right. Leave it to me."

The error came from the East York outlet... Lawrence's. I had my doubts about that young man and now this. Was he too much of a dreamer for such a challenging profession? Was he too weak to ride herd on his staff?

Was he too weak to take on Yasmin? While a man always needed to say "yes" to his wife, he also needed to be as strong as she was so that he could find an hour here or there to escape, have an outlet and stay sane. Something like boating or wood carving or a mistress.

He also needed the strength to challenge her when necessary. Not say *no* or anything stupid like that, but to gently guide her while making her think it was all her own idea.

Could Lawrence do that? If not, Yasmin would surely tire of him and divorce him. Then, not only would I never hear the end of it from her mother, but I'd have to pay for yet another wedding!

I ruminated on this as I drove to the Four Seasons and picked up the suit from the penthouse. I apologized profusely to the gentleman who seemed like a butler but was wearing a cashmere robe. One can never tell these days.

LAWRENCE

"This would never have passed my personal quality control," Azad told me.

"Yes, you're right," I said, agreeing with him, good practice for how I would speak to Yasmin, who I'd hardly seen in weeks.

"You must be passionate about this job, young man. You must see it as your service to humanity. Your life's mission! Is that how you see it?" He asked, mopping his brow.

"Um…" I tried to think of what to say that would please him.

"And you must be passionate about Yasmin! I need to see your passion!" he said, his face close to mine.

"You're right sir, I'm sorry sir," I said.

He relaxed and backed away from me, looking at me up and down. "Good. Good." Then he handed me a piece of wood and a knife. "Start with Gandhi, he's the smallest."

YASMIN

I had fallen deeply and eternally in love with Rashid. I loved him more than I loved myself! I'd never felt that way before.

I loved how forceful he was, not some namby-pamby poof who said yes to everything—I hated that. I loved how he took control as a lover, looking into my eyes and telling, not asking. Normally I hated it when anyone told me what to do but I wanted this from him— I wanted to lose control.

But I did wish I could control one thing— I wished I could make him tell me he loved me! I said it to him after each orgasm, of which there were many even in a single afternoon.

He had never said it, not even once. He'd say weird shit like, "te amo." Huh? What did he want with ammo, this was Canada! Once he said, "मैं तुमसे प्यार करता हूँ" and I had no fucking idea what he meant and was orgasming too hard to form words to ask!

Boo loves me. I will marry him.

DAVID

The next morning there was a flurry of texts on my phone. I read Diane's, "Sorry to hear about it. Just know I'd be happy to work with you again, even if nobody else will." Robert sent two cases of vodka with a note that read, "this always makes *me* feel better."

WTF?

The other texts said, "Sorry," or "Bad break," or "Oscar's a fucktard." The last one I read was from my lawyer, Jan. It included a link to *Variety.com* - a full page ad that read:

DEAR HOLLYWOOD:
DAVID SILVER HAS BEEN FIRED
FOR BEING A USELESS PIECE OF SHIT
YOU'D BE CRAZY TO WORK WITH HIM.
LUCKILY, TROLLHEIM WILL BE A HIT
THOUGHT THE UNIQUE CREATIVE VISION
OF OSCAR-WINNER J. MICHAEL CONNASSE

Just like that. All caps. On the facing page was an article about how I'd been released from my role of executive producer for, and I quote, "Running over time, over budget and creating a cut so useless that J. Michael and his award-winning team of editors will need to work tirelessly night and day to make the release."

"J. Michael stated, 'I am personally making this mess into a gorgeous, moving film for the entire family that we predict will be the biggest hit of this and every future holiday season!'"

I called Jan. "Don't worry, David, everyone knows Oscar's a psycho, and no matter what happens with the film, Universal still has to pay you. You'll keep Exec Producer credit unless you want it removed. I'm drawing up a defamation suit against numbnuts and Universal for a hundred million dollars so they'll either shut up or pay up."

It didn't matter that everyone knew who and what Oscar was— Now the Jackass had my job. Worse, my name had publicly tarnished in front of everyone I might possibly work with in the future.

I was done.

I couldn't find my watch. Hiroto said he'd found it in the freezer, along with my underwear. I had no idea how that happened but the cold boxers were soothing as I stood on the balcony, looking over the edge.

I wasn't actually thinking about jumping, I just wished I could fly. Away. Forever.

TEDD

Poor Davey. He needed moral support and I was clearly the only one who actually cared about him.

DAVID

Hiroto pulled me back from the edge, which felt like a familiar gesture.

"Shell and I are there for you, Mr. David."

"You can just call me *David*."

"Just give it to me, it's my little joke."

"OK, Mr. Hiroto."

"No, it doesn't work that way," he frowned.

"Thank you. I am lucky to have you two in my life because otherwise... I don't know what I would do."

"Yes you do," Hiroto said, staring into my eyes as if trying to communicate telepathically.

"You have beautiful eyes," I told him, not understanding his unspoken message, whatever it was.

"Last night, in the tub, you told me."

"Oh, no, I'm sorry for whatever I might have said," I pulled back, embarrassed, noticing how warm my boxers had become.

"You said that *Trollheim* should be *a series*."

I felt an exploding sensation inside me, like the one I'd had last night, and I would have thrown up if I'd had anything left in my system to throw up. Instead, I gave Hiroto a big kiss. On the mouth. I mean, why not. He had lovely lips.

TARSEM

I'D HAD A TRANSCENDENT EXPERIENCE, SEEING THE UNIVERSE IN ALL ITS COLOURFUL, ENERGETIC GLORY! THE WORLD WAS LUMINOUS. I WAS LUMINOUS.

THE NEXT MORNING I FELT LIKE I'D BEEN SAT ON BY AN ELEPHANT. I HAD A SOAPY TASTE IN MY MOUTH THAT REMINDED ME OF WHEN MY MATA WASHED MY MOUTH OUT WITH LUX SOAP FOR HAVING SAID I WAS GOING TO MAKE MOVIES IN HOLLYWOOD. SHE WANTED ME TO BE A PHARMACIST. TROLLHEIM WAS MY BIG CHANCE TO SHOW HER I HAD MADE IT.

BUT NOW I FEARED I HAD FAILED.

JUST THEN, DAVID BURST INTO THE BATHROOM WHILE I WAS PEEING. I WAS SHOCKED AND MADE RATHER A MESS, INCLUDING ON HIS FEET WHEN HE SPUN ME AROUND AND GAVE ME A BIG HUG

AND SAID, TOO LOUDLY AND CLOSE TO THE HEARING AID IN MY LEFT EAR, "YOU ARE A GENIUS!"

DAVID

I'd been too excited to wait.

While Tarsem wiped up the bathroom mess, I told him my brilliant idea! His response was, "I must take a shower now, may we discuss this in a few minutes, David?" He was always so polite.

I sat on the bed outside the bathroom, eating a breakfast burrito because I was ravenous.

When he emerged from the bathroom I offered him half the burrito. He declined, reminding me he was a vegan. Hiroto, who never seemed to forget anything, had already ordered him vegan banana pancakes.

Over breakfast we discussed where we could break each episode. It was all falling into place.

I asked Jan to look over Robert and Diane's contract to make sure this would work. Because their contracts only referred to "the work" and never specified the format or lengths, we were clear to proceed.

I called Oscar. "Motherfucker!"

"Got that job at Starbucks yet? No, well, I'm so sorry for you," he laughed.

"Figured out what to do with the edit yet?" There was silence on the line.

"J. Michael is working on it." Oscar announced.

"I'll bet there's a lot of Klingon in it," I chided him. He cleared his throat. "I've got the solution that'll not only work, it'll make *you* look like a genius."

There was a long pause, "Go on," he said, flatly.

"Oh, I'm not going to tell you, asshole. I'm going to fix it for you. Once you rehire me."

OSCAR

David was a putz, but if he actually had a solution to the mess he himself made then I wanted to hear it, because J. Michael's cut was incomprehensible. Literally.

"OK, asshole," I told him. "I will, but only because now I can blame you a second time."

DAVID

I had only one other demand, that he place a full-page retraction in *Variety,* one that I would write.

DEAR HOLLYWOOD
DAVID SILVER IS A GENIUS*

That was all in huge type. But at the bottom, in almost unreadable small print, he'd added something I hadn't written: *And so am I, Oscar Kremnitz.*

Text to Oscar: It's an 8 episode series. *You're welcome*, schmuck.

OSCAR

This is why *I am* a genius: because I know how to motivate the talent!

Got a bidding war going between Amazon, Netflix and Apple. Genius!

LEIF

David called to say *Trollheim* is now a series. I am happy, because my entire family shares one Netflix account—and because I get a bonus, which is good, because I didn't know how expensive bathroom fixtures were.

I am writing a new screenplay about remodeling a townhouse.

TARSEM

"You don't have to hold yourself together," David told me,

"Because I've got your back."

He sat with me the entire time we re-edited.

I felt this series was my mission in life.

TEDD

"Surprise!"

DAVID

Tedd was sprawled out on my bed, naked. Shit, he always looked good naked.

I wanted to be angry but was more surprised and curious. "How'd you get in here?"

"Hi, Davey," he growled seductively. "I told the nice girl at the front desk that I'm your husband."

"Ex-husband," I clarified.

He smiled, "That's just two little letters."

"Two letters and a dash!"

"*Us* is just two letters too," he said, biting a *Vosges Haut Chocolat* truffle in half, licking his lips and placing the other half in my mouth. Damn! "As always, I'm the one who shows up when you need someone the most," he said, sweetly. I'd forgotten how sweet he could be, and salty, like the bacon chocolate truffle that filled my mouth.

"I don't *need* you now," I told him, truthfully, which only made me *want* him more.

"Well, you needed me yesterday when I saw the first ad and I immediately got on a plane. That shows how much I care."

He looked so fucking great sprawled out on the bed like that. It was hot that he'd thoughtfully taken off the bedspread which he knew I felt harbored other people's worst germs.

"This is the big break I've always wanted for you," he whispered as if revealing a secret. "I've always believed in you, haven't I?"

Yes, he always had. Even when I was writing talking dog movies. Even when he read that ad and thought I might never work again.

"I've always been there for you haven't I?" He was starting to glisten, damn him!

"Not always..." I said to try to snap myself out of his spell.

"I made one mistake in 22 years. I know we can get over that." I was going to argue when he pulled me close, pulled down my pants and maneuvered my cock into his mouth.

I started to push him away, but it felt too good and right now all I could think of was the happy times that we had spent together. One thing led to another. And another. Some involving chocolate in deliciously unexpected ways.

I momentarily worried about getting chocolate on the sheets, but then lost myself in the sensation, the memories of our life together, the epicurean pleasure and the carnal knowledge of *him* wanting *me again*.

TEDD

I played his body like an instrument. Blowing, fingering, gliding, tickling. Staccato. Legato.

He knew just how to play me, too, and the time apart made me appreciate how well he knew me. Our vibrations harmonized to an explosive crescendo.

It was a symphonically good fuck.

DAVID

Tedd fell asleep immediately after he came. He always did that. I lay there, looking at him. Inspecting him. His hips were narrow. His dick was wide. Lucky bastard. Though his eyes were closed, I could remember his effortlessly blue eyes.

He had always been there for me in his own way. He'd always come home to me, in his own way. I'd never questioned how lucky I was to have him.

But I'd also never thought about how lucky he was to have me.

I got out of bed, dressed quietly, and took the elevator to the lobby where it was silent and still in the middle of the night, nobody even at the front desk. I went outside in the chilly night air and wondered what to do next with my life.

I could write with Tedd around. But had I ever written anything great with him around? Then again, could I write anything great even without him around?

More than that, did I want him around?

I thought about taking the elevator up to the penthouse and having Shelli smother me with her breasts. They were worse ways to go. But I needed to think.

Yet all this thinking was like a verbal fog machine in my head to keep me from feeling what I had loved and lost. Lu.

I pulled out my phone and searched for his name. *That's when I saw the wedding announcement* in my email. He'd told me he'd never been with a woman and now he was marrying one—his best friend.

Tedd had been my best friend. Hadn't he? We were basically children when we met. I'd lived more of my life with him than without him.

I wished Lu and Yasmin well with all my heart. I hoped he would be happy.

Me? I'd fucked up. Lu was gone. No amount of longing was going to bring him back. I had to move on.

Tedd had always been my guy. Maybe he could be again.

TEDD

No matter what else happened, we'd always worked in bed. Sex always reconnected us even if I couldn't help needing connection with other men, too. I was always very social.

I woke up, surprised Davey was gone. Still, it was a relief. I'd gotten used to sleeping alone. At home there was a daybed in his office for guests—I could sleep there—Make his office *my* room so I could focus on *my* creative work.

Now that I'd gained a few pounds, I saw that Davey was right when he said bigger guys needed clothes, too. I could create a new line called *Living Large,* "for the man with something extra!"

There was plenty of room in the master bedroom for Davey's desk, if he was still writing anymore.

I was determined to make this work.

SHELLI

Shit. Shit in a bucket. Shit in a basket of puppies. Shit shit shit shit shit.

David brought Tedd up to the penthouse for cocktails. I was civil. I invited Tedd out to the balcony for a "heart-to-heart" talk where I told him, as sweetly as possible, that if he hurt David again I knew people who knew people. Either this was too subtle or he was too stupid, as his reply was, "That's nice, I know people, too." So I had to be more obvious, "If you fuck with David I will make sure you never fuck *anything* again as long as you live. Capeesh?"

He did seem to understand this, but with his handsome yet blank face it was always hard to tell.

In the past when Tedd was more svelte, I believe I could have thrown him over the railing and pretended it was an accident. But he'd put on some weight, which David liked but which made me unable to lift him (and trust me, I tried, in the guise of a hug).

I thought my dear, sweet, meshugenah David was over this yutz. But no. He was giggling like a schoolgirl. It was nauseating. I loved him but was disgusted with him.

HIROTO

I TOOK DAVID ASIDE AND ASKED HIM IF HE WAS SURE THIS WAS A GOOD IDEA.

HE SAID, "OH, HIRO, I'VE ALWAYS LOVED HIM AND I JUST FORGOT THAT."

I SAID, "ARE YOU SURE HE'S NOT JUST A GREAT LAY? I MEAN, YOU KNOW I KNOW HE IS. REMEMBER THAT?"

HE KISSED MY CHEEK AND SAID, "I APPRECIATE YOUR CONCERN, HIRO, BUT I'M A GROWN ASS..." I STOPPED HIM RIGHT THERE AND SERIOUSLY CONSIDERED LOCKING HIM IN THE LINEN CLOSET.

DAVID

Shell and Hiro were so happy for us!

DORY AKA PEMA SITA

No matter how enlightened I might become, I was still a human being with feelings.

I got this text from David: Dear Pema. All is well. I am back with Tedd.

I threw my phone on the ground and jumped up and down on it. It made the most satisfying cracking sounds.

Did David learn nothing from me? I felt like a failure.

I know, I know, this was not my decision, much less my fault. David was a fool and from what he said, Tedd had a big dick.

I was glad I no longer had a phone.

I was glad I was celibate.

ZORN

So the idiot was back with Tedd. He wasn't actually happy and he also wasn't writing. Buzz. Wrong answer!

Must it always require my divine intervention to get this supposedly mature man to write, much less see the light? Apparently.

I remembered that working with humans was hard 400,000 years ago but I'd forgotten how illogical and frustrating they were.

DAVID

I know, I know, it seemed foolish to let him back into my life, but love wasn't logical.

Tedd was staying with me and it was like our second honeymoon. I'm deliriously happy. Or at least delirious, though I thought I was happy, or would be once it started to feel real.

YASMIN

Rashid lightened my hair to a platinum silver. I felt like a new woman. I told him I loved my new look. I told him I loved him.

He said, "Je t'aime." Huh? He had to jet to the Thames in London? I didn't care if it was Posh Spice, no other client should have been more important than me?

I thought I was going to die.

LAWRENCE

Yasmin came in late, as usual, and her beautiful black hair was now what she called platinum. I would have described it as more of a pewter alloy.

She said she was so happy but her eyes were red. When I asked her about it she claimed it was the chemicals from the color. Yasmin was very confusing.

I did not need to do such hair coloring as I started noticing gray hairs at my temples which I would call sterling or argentium.

As the wedding approached, she was too busy to do the planning, so I had been choosing colors, selecting flowers, doing cake tastings, and designing the invitations.

Inspired by all the silver happening around me, I selected a silver white winter theme. It was going to be beautiful. I should have been happy, shouldn't I?

But silver made me think of David's last name... and how I liked to play with the curly locks in his beard. I closed the door to my office and jacked off one final time and thought I'd never think about him again. Ever.

Except after, in that warm glow, I was still thinking about him.

TEDD

David has asked me to go to the monastery because he hasn't heard from Pema Sita who used to be Dory. Does he mean Dory transitioned to Pema? I guess I'd see.

I was making great progress on my *Living Large* line, especially in my brilliant use of slimming spandex panels. The dark material broke up the mass of a larger body, and the spandex comfortably held the body into place while offering breathing room for buffets.

TARSEM

Before I returned home to Mumbai, I gave David an antique jade cabochon worry stone with Ganesha carved into it. It had helped me through this difficult but wondrous time, and I saw that David was deeply confused.

I told him, "You gave me a priceless gift with this opportunity, my friend. So I give you this priceless gift: Ganesha. He is the remover of obstacles and brings good luck. He is also the patron of art and writers."

Now I would go back home and make my passion picture, an intimate autobiographical film about a poor boy who is taught to love by a mouse.

DAVID

Tarsem gave me a beautiful gift. He said, "Keep it in your pocket and touch it to remind you what is precious to you."

I asked if I could produce his mouse movie and he laughed, "You are a writer! You don't want to produce. Stop convincing yourself that your thoughts are true. Listen to your heart."

He gave me a very warm and tight hug for such a petite man. I cried, because his gift was beautiful, his words were beautiful, and because this beautiful project was finally done and I could relax at last.

DORY AKA PEMA SITA

I had never met Tedd, and yet I recognized him immediately when I saw him on the grounds, talking to a young monk, Rhu.

Rhu laughed, which is permitted in our silent monastery, because laughter, like tears, is the language of enlightenment.

Seeing Tedd caused me to deeply investigate the possibility that one of the roads to enlightenment could come from knowing who to kick in the balls.

TEDD

This commanding woman walked right up to me, looking me in the eyes and asked, "Are you Tedd?"

I asked her, "Are you Pema Sita and what happened to Dory?"

I didn't see it coming.

DORY AKA PEMA SITA

I kicked him in the balls, honestly feeling with my whole heart that he needed this.

Rhu looked concerned, but I simply raised my right arm as if to say, "It's OK" and he nodded like he understood, but also took three steps back away from me.

RHU

!

HARRY

!...

Rhu was gesturing like crazy. I had no idea what he was saying or trying to say.

I gave him some tea and we breathed together.

A man I recognized as Tedd from photos on David's phone stumbled in, crying.

I gave him some tea and we breathed together.

DORY AKA PEMA SITA

That was the final release I needed. I could let go of anger. I could let go of words. I could let go of my old life and focus on Vinaya, the basket of discipline.

I drank some tea. Turned off the lights and basked in the starlight.

TEDD

The monastery was the most peaceful place I had ever been. And I loved the fabric they wove for their robes.

Robes. That was it. Free-flowing. Traditionally masculine in an Arabic way. No worry about body shape or size or buffet bloating.

Rhu and Harry gave me a tour of the abbey. When I sat at a weaving loom something clicked inside my head. I heard it. At first I thought maybe it was a stroke because I saw those cartoon stars circling my head. But no, it was enlightenment.

DAVID

Tedd didn't come home from the monastery. My room seemed much calmer without him here yammering on about spandex.

I bundled up and lay on the balcony chaise, looking at the stars.

ZORN

Now was my chance.

DAVID

I couldn't go to sleep, so I wrote:

EXT. VIEW OF EARTH FROM SPACE - DAY/NIGHT/OUT
HERE WHO CAN TELL?

The entire planet seems to shake on its axis.

ZOOM IN ON SEX STADIUM

50,000 people, naked, sleeping.

Zorn sits on the dais, eating a mozzarella cheese
stick.

>   ZORN
>   I'd forgotten how much I love these
>   things.

Norz hands Zorn a viewscreen with images of
stadiums in London, Berlin, Moscow, Beijing,
Caracas, Mogadishu, Delhi, Sydney and
DisneyWorld.

>   NORZ
>   Their DNA is now reprogrammed in 56
>   countries around the globe. Peace
>   shall prevail.

As the sleeping people awake, they begin to cry,
weep and wail, their tears a day-glo green that

```
causes their faces to dissolve, then drip down
turning bodies into small piles of dust.

                    ZORN
        Back to the drawing board.
```

ZORN

What the fuck? I didn't tell him to write that. No!
Everyone is supposed to be happy. Peaceful. They're
supposed to be fucking peaceful!!!

DAVID

```
As the sleeping people awake, they begin to cry,
weep and wail, their tears a day-glo green that
causes their faces to dissolve, then drip down
turning bodies into small piles of dust.

        ZORN
Back to the drawing board.
```

I felt it was wrong as soon as I typed it, but I couldn't help it. I
didn't know why, but tears had been streaming down my face and
it just ended up on the page.

```
...As the sleeping people awake, they look
around. Black, white, Asian, Latino, Aboriginal,
East Indian...
```

I stopped typing.

In the distance I heard church bells chime..

YASMIN

I was throwing up all morning. Mother said it was normal during pregnancy. Father said it was nerves. They were both wrong. It was the idea of spending the rest of my life with Boo. Look, I loved the boy, he was a sweetheart, but he shouldn't have forced me to marry him.

I know he was brokenhearted about David, and I took pity on him but how could I give up my life for him? Still, he was my best friend. I wanted to talk with him about it—but I didn't want to hurt his feelings.

Oh, fuck, the wedding dress my mother insisted on was hideous. I looked like a parade float.

But I could not disappoint mother and father and Boo. I would martyr myself for their happiness.

I was too good of a person.

LAWRENCE

My uncle Fareed made my wedding suit. He called it "dove gray" but I felt it was more of a Molybdenum colour. He said, "I am very happy for you," then started crying.

FAREED

I started crying before I got to the words I had practiced on the plane, "...Are you sure you want to do this? Pretending to love a woman didn't work for me and I don't think it will work for you."

I nearly choked on the candied violet pastille I had in my mouth. Lawrence kissed me on the cheek and I thought, "Shut up, Fareed, maybe he will be happy this way." I went to sit with brother Bashir, in the church.

LAWRENCE

The wedding suit fit like it was made for me, because it was.

Still, my waistcoat felt like a straitjacket.

Even more painful was the barbed wire necklace under my silver bow tie to remind me of why I was doing this. For Yasmin.

I felt so alone—but once I married Yasmin, my best friend, I would never be lonely again.

AZAD

As her father, I could smell Yasmin's problem a mile away. It wasn't coming from the retching noises in her bathroom, or the fact that her wedding dress was so tight now it barely closed.

Luckily, Rashid, the hairdresser, arrived. I liked the cut of his jib. I also liked that he had a calming effect on Yasmin and her mother so I could calm down.

I knew gay hairdressers had this effect on women and had seen it when my wife returned from the salon.

I checked my watch and if we didn't leave soon we were going to be late for our own wedding. Yet Yasmin was nowhere to be found... oh wait, I found her in her walk-in closet, kissing Rashid on the mouth. I was shocked, shocked!

"How dare you kiss my daughter," I said indignantly. "You are a gay man, stick to your own kind!"

"He was just applying my lipstick, father, this is the way it's done these days," Yasmin said, indignant right back.

Rashid nodded, and he did, indeed, have lipstick on which made him very pretty.

"I'm sorry, I do not understand modern beauty rituals," I apologized because I was so good at apologizing and it was easier than wondering what the implications of this so-called ritual were.

YASMIN

Rashid had his chance. He never said "love," he only spouted a bunch of gibberish in languages I didn't know. I didn't tell him this, because I shouldn't have to tell him this—he should have known! I wiped the lipstick off his gorgeous full lips with the handkerchief mother had given me in case I cried at the wedding. I would cry, all right.

TEDD

For the first time I could remember, I wasn't horny. That was the effect the monastery had on me. Rhu and Harry were sexy as fuck, and in the past the three of us would have been writhing, naked and sticky in the apple cider barrel.

But I didn't feel the need to touch them—our spiritual connection was so much deeper.

Weaving at the loom shocked me: How tactile the thread was as I wove it into fabric; The way it engaged my entire body in a completely sensual way; my eyes watching the colorful thread weave into patterns, my arms and torso pulling back on the bar, my hands working the shuttle; my legs and feet pressing the pedals to raise and lower the warp threads. It was hard, physical work, like going to the gym but with something tangible to show for it!

I'd spent my life seeking carnal pleasures and here was all I needed, all encompassing—with a result I could share, hold in my hands, stroke and caress, and sew into garments that would caress others.

I saw a life ahead of me, weaving fabric, sewing robes by hand for the abbey and using an Etsy page to sell them and raise funds for the monks. Bliss.

DAVID

I heard the church bells again. I'd never heard them before but now they were deafening.

I looked at my phone. It was Sunday. The day of Lawrence's wedding.

I felt like I had a rock of regret in my digestive track, moving slowly through me.

I put on my black tuxedo, the one I wore to my movie premieres.

I convinced myself I would be happy for Lu. I would support him in whatever he chose because this is what you did when you *loved* someone.

Oh, no!

SHELLI

Hearing uncertainty in David's voice, I told him in no uncertain terms, "You are not going through this alone, my little love. You are supporting Lu and we are supporting you."

HIROTO

I brought the Rolls around. David looked quite handsome in his tux but his face was so pale I was afraid he was going to be sick again. I had Shelli sit in the front with me, just in case.

The church was a brutalist gray concrete pile that looked like a factory with a cross on it.

Shell and I each took one of David's arms as we led him in. He saw Lu and collapsed into the last pew.

DAVID

I was fine. Absolutely fine. I was there to support the man I loved... love... loved.

Even though Tedd hadn't returned from the monastery, I figured he was and always would be my man—for whatever that was worth, because I also knew he'd never really be mine.

But that was OK. Totally OK! We were a modern gay couple and that's how it worked, though when my friends had open relationships they at least talked about it first.

I rubbed the jade worry stone in my pocket and thought, "Please Ganesha... please remove the obstacles to my happiness."

I was not going to spoil Lu's happiness with Yasmin. Absolutely, positively, 100% not.

LAWRENCE

I didn't know anybody in Toronto who didn't work at the dry cleaner, so Azad was my best man, holding onto my arm like a tourniquet as if to prevent me from escaping.

DAVID

99% not.

LAWRENCE

I wasn't going anywhere—my parents were here, as happy as I have ever seen them.

BASHIR

I never thought I would live to see this day!

FAREED

I had hoped I would never see the day when my good gay nephew would try to go straight. Brother Bashir was crying tears of joy. I was just crying.

YASMIN

"Boo is my best friend. I love him," I repeated silently to myself. My mother thought I was praying, which I was, in a way.

"Boo will be a good father to our babies and will raise them to know right from wrong, like my father did."

Was I hyperventilating? I felt dizzy.

"Rashid has never said he loves me. I must move on from my childish crush and be the woman and mother I want to be."

The dress was suffocating me.

The dress! I called for Esme, my maid of honor. She had a bottle of red wine and the real dress I'd picked out with Boo. I poured the wine down the poofy white dress and stared at the red stain spread.

Esme shook me, "What's wrong with you, girl? You gotta get out of that cake topper and into your real dress."

She unbuttoned the 72 buttons in the back and I let the dress fall to the floor, like my hopes and dreams.

I fought to get into the nude lace dress. Esme couldn't get it zipped up the back and used safety pins to close it. "It's OK, Yasmin, your veil will hide it."

Just then mother came in and exclaimed, "What are you wearing???" Esme quickly explained the "accident" as she ushered mother out into the church.

I turned to the mirror. I looked like a lacy cow, though my arms did look sexy.

LAWRENCE

The organ music started. Azad released my arm so he could stand with Yasmin. I'd yet to see her today, but upon remembering her pewter hair I feared it would not coordinate well with the lace of her dress. This would almost certainly put her in a fowl mood which made me even more nervous than I already was.

Uncle Fareed put his arms around my shoulder and gently asked, "Are you sure, bebe?"

"No, Uncle. I am not sure of anything other than organic chemistry."

"It is *not* too late to stop this now," he patted my back.

"I would rather hurt myself than hurt her."

"That's no way to go through life—I know," Fareed whispered.

"I lost the one man I loved, so what's the point?" I choked.

"Love is never lost—if you keep looking for it."

I saw the minister nod his head at us. I started walking like a robot—staring straight ahead. I was afraid if I looked into the eyes of the people watching they might know what was going through my head—*Escape! Escape!*

DAVID

Lu looked so beautiful. He always looked beautiful. I was so angry with myself that I wanted to scream. I rubbed the worry stone so much it was getting hot.

I couldn't look, I put my head on Shelli's bosom and quietly sobbed, "I have lost my true love, so what's the point?"

"It's always darkest before the dawn..." she said, stroking my hair. "...and all that crap. You know what I've gone through—and survived. You're lucky—At least Lu's alive."

I looked up. He was alive, and I could see him shaking from all the way back here.

MINISTER

Ah, the wedding march started. Grooms were always nervous but I'd never seen one this nervous. They all tried to smile and look happy but they instinctively knew what was coming. The honeymoon. The in-laws. The kids. The fights. The mortgage. The schools. I saw it over and over: the happy couple would bring their beloved child to preschool, together. By first grade it was mostly just mothers bringing the kid. By second grade, there she was, sans wedding ring.

I hoped the groom read the information sheet I sent to all brides and grooms suggesting they wear incontinence undergarments. Just in case.

It was a stupidly long walk down this football-field-length aisle, a problem as too many brides and grooms tripped or fainted along the way.

Finally, here she was. Showtime!

YASMIN

Jesus, that was a long walk, especially in these stilettos. Boo looks like he's going to pass out. I hope he read the sheet about waterproof underwear.

DAVID

I remember my wedding to Tedd. We'd been together for 20 years and gay marriage just had been made legal. I told Tedd we should finally get married.

He said, "We don't want marriage to change the love we share!"

Turns out he was right. It changed it. Not that I was against marriage, but...

MINISTER

"...It is not something to be entered into lightly..."

DAVID

It's not something to be entered into lightly...

MINISTER

"...for better, for worse, for richer, for poorer, in sickness and in health, to love and to cherish, till death do us part..."

LAWRENCE

I'm dying.

YASMIN

I'm dead inside—like my mother.

DAVID

This is killing me.

MINISTER

If there is anyone in attendance who has cause to believe that this couple should not be joined in marriage, you may *speak now* or *forever hold your peace.*

SHELLI

Good on the minister for leaving a nice long pause here.

I stared hard at David.

ZORN

OK, Human. It's now or never. You love Lu—get off your ass!

DAVID

I jumped. Up. Standing. My right arm above my head, holding the worry stone.

MINISTER

Uh, oh!

ZORN

SAY SOMETHING!!!

DAVID

Suddenly I knew what I needed to say.

"I DO!" I shouted.

MINISTER

Everybody gasped. I just sighed—all bets were off. Literally, I had a bet going about this couple with Father McIntyre.

DAVID

"I mean, I OBJECT!" I yelled, hearing a whoosh of fabric as everyone turned to look at me.

RASHID

"I DO TOO!" I SAID, PISSED OFF THAT THIS OTHER GUY HAD STOLEN MY THUNDER. I'D WAITED FOR THIS POINT IN THE SERVICE BECAUSE IT WAS GOING TO MAKE A KICK-ASS VIRAL VIDEO AND GREAT PUBLICITY FOR MY NEW "SALON YASMIN," BUT THIS JERK SPOILED THE MOMENT. DAMN—I STILL WANTED TO MARRY HER.

YASMIN

"What the fuck, Rashid, why didn't you fucking say something before fucking now?" I blurted out—so glad I was wearing those undergarments.

LAWRENCE

"I DO, TOO!" I heard myself yelling—to David.

MINISTER

I'm sorry, son, but the groom can't object.

LAWRENCE

"I just did! I mean, come on, look at that guy!" I said, pointing to Rashid.

"And look at *my* guy!" I cried, running towards David who was running up the ridiculously long aisle.

Rashid was faster and had already reached Yasmin. She jumped into his arms, her weight causing them both to fall on the floor.

I jumped into David's arms and he kissed me. Right in front of God and everybody.

FAREED

There is a God, even in a Christian church!

LAILA

I punched Bashir, "I told you our son would never marry a woman— You owe me a trip to Greece!"

BASHIR

She did tell me. Hello, Mykonos!

SHELLI

I turned to Hiroto, "Now's your chance, too, bucko!"

HIROTO

"WILL YOU MARRY ME?"

MINISTER

This was a first—I'd never had three couples standing before me at once.

I flipped through the pages of the service, looking for where to start.
Fuck it.

"Do you... people take this... person to be your lawfully wedded... mate... till death do us part?"

YASMIN & RASHID

(Grunting noises while making out)

SHELLI & HIROTO

You bet your ass!

DAVID & LAWRENCE

We do we do we do we do!

MINISTER

I now pronounce you husbands and wives—and husband! You may kiss... each other.

YASMIN

It's about fucking time!

SHELLI

God, I love Hiroto! As we kiss, I silently pray nothing bad happens to him. Please, God, please, please, please. I'll donate 10 million dollars to the church, OK? Just answer this one prayer!

HIROTO

I'M SO HAPPY I COULD DIE! BUT I WOULDN'T DO THAT TO SHELL. NO—
WE WILL HAVE A LONG, HAPPY LIFE TOGETHER!

DAVID

I am laughing and crying at the same time. What a beautiful
shitshow.

Lu's face beams back at me. We kiss again and I hold him tight,
grabbing his ass.

LAWRENCE

David kisses me passionately.

Time had stopped, but now it all comes rushing at me, the sound, the flower
smells, and David's beautiful face!

I feel his hand on my ass, and I squeeze his ass back.

I've never been happier in my entire life.

DAVID

I've never been happier in my life. Oh, my God, I want to write!

➤ ABOUT THE AUTHOR

An internationally-recognized best-selling author, MoMA has called Daniel's work "truly unique." He's developed plays with the *Kennedy Center Playwriting Intensive, Naked Angels Theater,* and *The Actor's Centre* in London.

His 8 books have sold over 300,000 copies, he has three produced screenplays to his credit, and he's written over 600 short stories currently featured in his popular story podcast.

Daniel created and wrote the book on his *Write in the Now* writing practice. He teaches writers and artists to discover endless ideas, eliminate writer's block, find passion in their projects, and get to the very heart of their work.

See all his work here:

WWW.WILL-HARRIS.COM